Tales of the

Unquiet Gods

Also by David E. Pascoe
Baptism By Fire

Tales of the Unquiet Gods

A Collection

by

David E. Pascoe

Scribe's Blood Press

Copyright © 2016 by David E. Pascoe

Previously published as:

Shadow Hands Copyright © 2015 by David E. Pascoe
Fallen Knight Copyright © 2015 by David E. Pascoe
Heal Thyself Copyright © 2015 by David E. Pascoe
By Hands and Knees Copyright © 2015 by David E. Pascoe
Wizard Training Copyright © 2015 by David E. Pascoe
Within Range Copyright © 2015 by David E. Pascoe

A Scribe's Blood Press Original
Www.scribesbloodpress.com

ISBN 978-0-9899053-7-4

Cover art and design by Sarah A. Hoyt

First edition, July 2016

For Sal, who poked and prodded and challenged.
Thank you, my friend.

And for David E. Snow,
Who fueled an early hunger for story.
I'm sorry you never got to see this, Mor Far.

SHADOW HANDS

LIGHTS FLICKERED OFF SLICK WHITE TILE, AND THE SHADOWS created reached for her. Mellie gulped and pushed off the sink. The bite of disinfectant mixed with human effluvia burned in her nostrils, but the only smell of which she was conscious was the reek of her own fear.

She'd seen the shadows take people.

She shuffled her feet, taking desperate care to not bump into anything or catch a heel on a crack in the bathroom floor. Heart bumping against ribs, Melody Devreux ached to turn and run, but it was all she could do to move slowly - oh, so slowly - backward. Cold comfort was the knowledge that the shadowy hands, full of too many fingers and each of them clawed, had never yet managed to reach her.

Her left hand clenched tight on the handle of her fiddle case, knuckles white. The usually-warm wood was worn smooth by the grip of more hands than she knew. When Daddy had still lived with them - back when they were happy - her parents had given her Grand-père Devreux's fiddle. Dad could sing beautifully in a rich baritone, but his fingers were roughened by his trade, and unfit to handle the precious instrument. He'd always said they'd never been as clever as hers anyway.

Mellie backed slowly through the door, almost bumping into a rumpled bag-woman pulling a small cart piled high with the detritus of the city. Mellie squeaked when the bag-woman snarled at her. The face full of noxious breath redolent of rotting teeth turned her stomach, and she stammered an apology and tried to become one with the wall as the half-crazed old street dweller stumped into the recently vacated ladies room.

She could feel herself starting to relax when she heard a muffled screech from inside the door. One often heard such noises in the city. Sounds that, upon first hearing them sounded strange and out of place. Sounds that upon reflection you knew as just a tire screeching on pavement, or a cat suddenly surprised, or maybe a passerby knocked off-balance.

But this wasn't that kind of sound. The bag-lady's shriek still rang in Mellie's ears, distorted and far more distant than the few feet and a door between them should have made it. Against her will and in league with her dread, Mellie's toe nudged the door open a bare inch.

The harsh, fluorescent lights flickered, baring the bag-lady's fallen handcart and scattered belonging. Of the old woman herself, there was no sign.

Until, by sick chance, her gaze was drawn to the wall opposite the door. A trick of the light gave the impression of a figure picked out in the tiles, all shades of white and grey. The bag-lady's eyes, no longer surly, but now more than half crazed, bored into Mellie's. Begging for help, pleading for release from the clawed shadow hands that pulled her deeper into the wall.

And then the lights flickered again. The old woman was gone completely. The door swung closed.

Mellie jammed her fist in her mouth, stifling to a whimper the scream trying to claw its way out of her throat. The wool of the gray half-gloves Mama'd knit her was rough as sandpaper against lips chapped from the chill air. Her skin - all over, not just that little bit exposed to the air - prickled, chilled from a cold not in the least physical. Despite the air that tried to suck the warmth from her, and in sharp contrast to the blood boiling as her fear-frenzied heart drove it through her veins.

Mellie's blue eyes swiveled feverishly in their sockets as her gaze skittered over the morning crowd in the subway station. Her desperation to escape faded the colors she saw to muted grays. The innocent looks people directed toward her took on ominous import.

She fled.

Movement seemed safer, though she didn't know why. She walked, her steps jerky and mechanical, up the stairs and onto the street. The sun's warm light on her skin slowed her racing pulse. The mute terror receded, granting Mellie a few snatched moments to remember.

She couldn't remember, anymore, a time when she hadn't seen the shadows reaching for her. Her fear was her constant, hated companion. She didn't understand why she wasn't gone as completely as the poor bag-lady, as disappeared as she believed her father had been.

Mama didn't understand her frantic insistence on sleeping with a light on, or why she refused to go out after dark. Yet she knew her mother harbored the same fear of the dark.

Dawn and twilight were the worst, those times when the light was just strong enough to cast shadows. Shadows that were solid, almost physical things. Tricks of the dark. Hungry tricks that stretched devouring fingers.

Mellie's wandering feet pulled her to a park. Not a big one, just a patch of grass with a few trees and bushes. The sun rained enough warmth and light down to ease her terror just a bit farther back into the dark of Mellie's mind.

With a glance at the sun's position in the sky, she decided she could chance a few songs. She stepped off the sidewalk, and the green of the leaves around her warmed her in ways her coat and sweater hadn't.

Despite the chill in the air, she slipped out of her shoes and worked her bare toes into the sparse grass. Squatting on her heels, her breaths slowing and deepening, Mellie laid her fiddle case on the ground. She was confident the cracked leather and wood of the case would stand up to the morning dew that lingered in the wan light of the autumn morning.

Carefully positioning the case so it was in the most direct light - and would consequently cast the least shadow - Mellie pulled at the old brass latches. The metal, bearing a fine patina from years of players hands, moved easily. A testament to her care, though the couple drops of oil were the least of the maintenance she lavished on her prize.

Passersby began to notice Mellie as a piece of the world that didn't - quite - fit into their routines. She drew curious glances as she opened the small door in the case and pulled out a cake of rosin. She swiveled the catches and removed her bow, taking a moment to ensure the threads were tight enough, but not too tight.

She took care to draw the bow across the rosin as she'd been taught by Grand-père before he, too, had gone. The sharp, pine scent woke memories of happier times, when her parents had taken a small Mellie Devreux out of the city and into the woods.

She'd been amazed to see so many trees in one place, and ran and ran through their brown and gray trunks. She'd loved the shadows in the forest, cast by a strong summer sun through bright green leaves. The light had barely filtered through, creating soft patches of deep, inky darkness. But a darkness full of warmth, and life, and - not security, by any means - but a kind of wild, passionate love.

But that was long ago, before grasping shadows began to pull people into walls.

She drew the bow swiftly a few times, and then carefully, inch by inch to ensure the whole length of the threads was thoroughly coated. She didn't plan to play long, but the tunes she loved best were the ones Grand-père had taught her, the folk songs of his native Normandy. When she played them, though, the Celtic wildness poured through the sprightly notes in a way that scared her just a little.

She put away the rosin, leaving the case open on the ground, and lifted the warm, wooden violin out of the cradling velvet of its case. She carefully checked the strings, plucking them quietly and tuning from what she heard.

With a deep breath, she leapt into tune. The notes tripped over each other as the bow slid back and forth across the strings. Mellie's eyes were shut tight in fierce concentration, trying to escape - if only for a moment - the deadly frightful place her world had become.

Trying, and succeeding. As music poured forth from her, spilling from her fingers, the terror faded. The shadowy claws disappeared from her her mind. Her pulse raced, yes, but from the fierce joy of creation. Melody loved making music. Mama used to joke that Mellie had gotten all the talent she'd never had. Now, she pushed it out of her hands, out her fingers and through her fiddle.

Even the sun seemed brighter through her closed eyelids.

Melody's music, redolent of wilderness, deep forests and the complex interplay of life, wrapped around the pedestrians walking past. Though she didn't know, couldn't know, none of these would feel the horror of dark, ethereal hands reaching out of black un-places to pull them from existence. Their hearts were buoyed up by the slender young woman standing barefoot in the grass, by her bewitching music.

Several even dropped money into her case as they went on their disparate ways. Busking was legal, though somewhat looked down upon.

Unless it was good.

Song flowed into song, and Melody played. She played to hold back the bone-gnawing, soul-staining fear. She played for the wild joy that gripped her and soothed her skittish heart. She played for the memory of her father and of Grand-père. Her fingers flashed as the notes became a cataract of sound.

An unseen observer wondered at her passion, at her power. He flipped a coin toward her case, and blessed her for the pleasure she'd brought him. The coin flew lazily through the air, scattering sunlight from its shiny surface as it tumbled through the air.

Mellie saw the glint of the coin through her eyelids, so bright was it. But she was consumed by her art, and unconscious of it.

Melody played until her fingers hurt and her heart didn't. She played until cold, gray buildings blocked the afternoon sun from her face. Her fears, now only a pale imitation of the consuming thing they'd been, made her skin prickle. She should be getting home.

Mellie bent to put away her fiddle, and started. Her case was full of money. Ones and grubby change, mostly, but as she sorted through it, she received another shock. Nestled among the legal tender lay a gold coin. Somehow, she knew the luster was genuine. It was no larger than the pad of one of her fingers, with an irregular edge. The figures on either face were worn into illegibility. She thought one might be a face, and the other some kind of animal. And the coin weighed heavy in her palm.

Thoughtful, Mellie shoveled the rest of the cash into her pocket and put her violin away, latching first the bow, and then the case itself with the remote detachment of long habit. She stood, and taking up her case in one hand - and with tiny, gold coin clenched tightly in the other - she slipped her shoes back on.

As she stepped off the grass, which seemed oddly greener and more vibrant than when she'd arrived in the little park, Melody Devreaux saw a shadowy hand reaching its slow scuttling way out of a storm drain a few feet distant.

Instead of the usual mind-blanking terror, she felt a hard knot of anger coalesce in her middle. She gripped her fiddle case in one shaking hand and the gold mystery coin in the other. Shaking in palpable rage now, instead of her earlier fear.

On an impulse so strong she couldn't resist it, Mellie whistled a few bars from her favorite song. The translucent black claw flinched, a bare inch away from an unknowing pedestrian's ankle. It writhed as she whistled and then began to shake itself apart, disintegrating before her eyes.

Barely believing it, Melody stared at the spot until the clawed member was completely gone. The same fierce joy she'd felt while playing wound through her heart. She had a way to fight back now.

Humming quietly to the world, Mellie turned and went home.

FALLEN KNIGHT

TOURNEY MARTIN HUDDLED AGAINST THE SIDE OF THE FLATIRON Building and shivered. He wasn't cold from the air: he didn't really feel that anymore. The chill gripping his guts and bones came from deep inside.

The creeping things had gotten Joe and Maddy.

He didn't know exactly when he'd started seeing real things. He saw stuff that wasn't there a lot. Usually things from his memories, but more and more – especially in the Down Below, under the streets – he saw stuff that shouldn't be.

Figures that couldn't possibly be human moved in the dark and the shadows. Teeth as long as his fingers, hair even longer, eyes big and pale yellow, shiny black skin like his best boot polish. And always he heard their murmuring, murmuring, like a conversation just too far away to understand. It sounded like gravel or ball-bearings poured into a huge metal bucket.

If that bucket wanted to pull the bones from your body.

Tourney shivered, despite the sunlight on his face. Daytime, and fresh air — fresh for the city, at least – and other people around seemed to help, to hold back the creeping dread. It was safer Down Below, usually. No cops to kick him along, or hipsters to judge him, or activists to try to help him better himself. Or worst of all – he snarled to himself – shrinks to make him think he was even crazier than he knew he was.

But.

People, his people, were going missing Down Below. Under the streets. In the dark. Most of the Down Below was dark, but it was starting to get scary. Really scary, like stuff whispering in your ear and then not being there when you turn around scary.

Three days ago he'd watched Joe Mutter and Mad Maddy walk into a deep, inky shadow. And then not walk out again. Joe's mutter was constant. That's why they called him Joe Mutter. The dark patch in the forgotten hallway Down Below had swallowed Joe and his constant companion Madeline, and then – for the first time since he'd met him – Tourney heard Joe's mutter stop. There'd been a kind of a sigh that faded off into silence.

Then a half-dozen pairs of little yellow spots came on in the dark. Like eyes. Looking at him. Tourn had left Down Below, and hadn't been back since. Lots of other street people were doing the same thing, he'd noticed.

After days on the surface, though, with the lack of good, safe sleep that came with it, he was starting to wonder if he'd been seeing things.

Again.

Tourn thought it had started sometime after coming home from the Sandbox and the suck. Life hadn't been kind, but he'd never asked it to. At almost six feet of cord and gristle under coffee-colored skin, Tourn had always found a place, even if he'd had to make it himself. That had been true in the Corps. It had been especially true after Mama left him and his father. His now-disjointed memories of childhood made Tourney think she hadn't been quite right in the head.

Maybe that's where he got it from.

The normal smells and sounds of the surface city were good things. Fried whatever with spices set his stomach to growling in a comfortingly normal way. Taxis' blatting honks and the cocktail-party-full-of-birds chatter of humanity pulled him back from the edge of his dis-ease. Somewhere nearby, some busker played music. The pleasant weight of the city – his city – gave Tourney space in his head.

To think. To remember.

Life in the Corps had been good for him. He'd made friends –

real friends – for the first time in his life. He'd proven good at important military things. Watching his buddies' backs. Keeping his nose clean. Drinking beer. His stutter, the bane of his childhood, had even gone mostly away.

And then That Night.

Tourney's fingers tightened until his ragged nails dug painfully into his skin where they were wrapped around his bent legs. He didn't feel it, though. He was someplace else. The comforting presence of the city vanished, and he was once again in the hot, dusty streets of a place halfway across the world.

The flashes from his muzzle illuminated brief stills of the action around Lance-corporal Martin. He'd always found it strange, the way his goggle and eye seemed to work against each other at night. Bright lights blinded the night vision goggle, while those same flashes showed his Mark One Eyeball what the goggle couldn't see. Of course, then his personal night vision was gone, and the eye not with a goggle had to adapt. Slowly. At the least the NVG got used to things pretty quickly. By now, the interplay was nearly instinctive.

He turned and dropped to a knee as movement from his right pulled at his strained consciousness. Finger squeezed trigger and a three-round burst ripped through a figure swathed in cloth and holding an AK.

"C'mon, Tourn," his squad leader, Sergeant Yves, yelled at him from a short way ahead. Martin obeyed, driving off his planted foot and pounding what passed for pavement in the slums his company was tasked to clear. Flashes from above and left told him somebody else was trying to kill his buddies.

He raised his carbine – there were many like it, but this one was his – taking care, as he'd been taught, not to sweep anybody he didn't want to shoot. Again, finger to trigger. Again, flashes and impact. No noise, though. It was weird how he could never remember hearing the sound of the fire of his own bullets. Just other people's.

He missed, he discovered as a figure leaned out of a second story window. Tourn crouched just as a strobe lit the blacker opening in the black wall. The distinct AK noise gave him hope, and the impact of bullets on the wall behind him told Martin his enemy didn't have nearly as much training as the USMC gave.

He switched the selector to semi-auto and squeezed off a round at the open window. And stepped quickly to the side, just in case. He wasn't trying to hit anything with that shot, just give the *muj* something else to shoot at. Tourn waited a beat, during which he set the selector back to burst fire, then ripped off three more rounds just as the figure leaned out again. The young lance-corporal sensed, rather than saw, an absence where he'd been shooting, and turned to follow his squad.

And froze.

Tourney's very soul screamed at what he saw. Nearly clear as day, hunched black figures struggled silently with his squad-mates. He got the impression of hair – or spines – and sharp, rending teeth, and knew he saw bright yellow-green eyes.

Time seemed to slow, and he knew what he'd see.

He'd seen it again. And again, and again.

Usually in his nightmares.

Sergeant Yves threw off one of the figures and fired a burst into – through? – its chest. The glare from the flashes lit up the entire street, and his goggle blanked, obedient to the bright light. Tourn saw a figure, a human figure, rise up from a rooftop and lift a tube to its shoulder. A tube with a pointed end.

As always, Tourn tried – God, he tried! – to alert his squad. He screamed, but no sound came out of his mouth. He ran toward them, but his feet move so very slowly. He could almost feel sharp-fingered hands holding him back, and somewhere he shivered. And all the figures turned to look at him. His squad-mates' eyes were filled with despair and the fore-knowledge of their own deaths, while the inhuman black figures laughed at Lance-corporal Martin's inability to save his friends.

The sharp crack-HISS of the rocket propelled grenade filled Tourn's mind. The flash of its ignition briefly lit up the night, and its trajectory blazed a trail across his vision. In the nightmare world of his memory, Tourn could actually see the warhead impact among his brothers.

The world went white.

Through the longest split-second of his life, through the thunder of the explosion and the remembered pain of a fist the size of a bus hitting him, Tourney Martin heard the fierce song of the busker.

There was a comfort in the notes. They wormed their way into his shattered soul, and their magic filled in some of the cracks. They warmed the chill in his bones. And when the notes faded away, the music inside him played on.

Tourn came back to the present in the same place he'd left it. Instead of the fear and despair he become accustomed to, however, he felt light. And, if not whole, at least less broken. Almost… free.

Tourn didn't know how long he'd been sitting trapped in his terror past, but his bones creaked as he pushed himself to his feet. Thrusting his arms over his head, he stretched. He was pretty sure every joint he possessed popped, one after another.

He moved out of the alleyway and slid into the foot traffic. He'd bathed a few days previous, so people didn't immediately shy away from him like they sometimes did. He'd learned early on to keep his arms and legs in, to occupy as little space as he could. Normal people didn't mind homeless head-cases, so long as you didn't intrude on their space. He moved forward, toward where he thought the music had been coming from. Something told him he needed to find the source.

If only to say thank you.

It was the first time in years a flashback hadn't ended with Tourney puking and shitting himself or hurting somebody while delirious. And that was worth everything.

As Tourn walked, his thoughts ranged. The actual blast had killed his squad. A flying piece of debris had impacted his helmet so hard he'd blacked out. When he came to – in a medical tent – he'd been unable to speak. Or move his head for the pain. Whiplash, concussion and the likelihood of further brain damage. Not to mention the cuts and scratches. They'd told him he'd been lucky to survive the blast, but he'd never seen it that way.

When it had come time for his after action report – as the only one left alive to do so – he'd dutifully written out what had happened. Typed, really, as he was still having trouble talking, and similar trouble with his handwriting. Which had never been that great, anyway.

The report had gone up his chain of command, and the shrinks had come back down. Are you sure you saw hairy monsters with glowing eyes, Lance-corporal? Wasn't it just maybe insurgents with some kind of mask on? Did Sergeant Yves do everything he should have? Did you?

By the time they were done with him, Tourney Martin didn't know what he'd seen. He remembered his squad in close-quarters battle with some kind of creatures. But had he actually seen that, or was it something the head wound had left him? Like the stutter that was worse than before he'd enlisted. And the headaches, and the nightmares where he watched his friends murdered again and again and again.

Tourney stopped in the middle of the sidewalk, something pinging his unconscious. He stood in front of a small park. It wasn't even a park, really, but a bit of manicured landscape in front of a building. A small crowd was in the process of dispersing, its individual bits going off about their own business. He slid his invisible way through the foot traffic until he stood on the grass.

The green, vibrant grass was odd for this late in the fall, especially in the city. Looking around, it came to Tourn that the people making their way past the little park were smiling. He realized he, himself, wasn't even wearing his near-constant scowl, and while it couldn't be said to be a smile, at least nobody was avoiding his gaze.

And then he looked down, and saw the footprints.

Somehow, the impressions of two bare feet had pressed down the grass just a short way from where he stood. As he bent down to look, he saw some of the blades stand back up. So, someone light. And right in front of the footprints was an oblong shape tamped down in the grass.

Urgency wrapped its fist around his heart. He didn't know why, but he had to find the player. He looked up, face fierce with purpose. Instinct honed by years spent on the street compelled him to movement, but Tourn beat it down. He needed intelligence.

He looked from face to face, searching for something to give him a clue. Not finding anything but the strangely gentle smiles on the faces of passersby, he looked down at the footprints again. Someone light. Small feet, too. Probably female.

He closed his eyes to think. It had always gotten him in trouble: first in school, and later in the Corps. His drill instructors always yelled at him when he did that to come up with an answer. Well, they'd always yelled at him, period. Him and all the other recruits. But it helped then.

And it helped now. Without all the visual distractions of the living city, Tourn could hear the song again. She – it had to be, with that voice – was humming the same tune he'd heard during his flashback. Jaunty. The word came unbidden to his lips. It was odd, though.

As he opened his eyes, the busyness of his city crowded in on him again. But he could still hear her humming cutting through the dull roar, as close as if she stood next to him. As though she was humming for him alone. Which was double weird to Tourney: no woman had paid him more than a moment's pity and a fiver in longer than he cared to think about.

Somehow knowing which way to turn – he didn't question a lot of things anymore – he followed the unknown songstress. His long legs ate up the pavement, his strides filled with a confidence he'd thought long, long vanished.

Something – a feeling, a kind of sense he hadn't known he had – told Tourn there was danger somewhere. Ahead? In the future? Nearby? He didn't know, just that he had something to do, and it involved the music maker.

Diesel and gasoline fumes, the smells of the street vendors – hot dogs, kabob, pickles, and roasted peanuts, just on one block – wrapped their fingers around him. The ever-present hum of the city – power lines, creaks and clanks, the chatter of the numberless humanity – beat on his ears. But not his mind, not today. Maybe not anymore. Her humming slipped inside his soul and smoothed some of the jagged parts.

He caught sight of her, he thought. A ways ahead, maybe half a block. Slim and short, she wore a dark-blue wool coat. What he'd called navy blue before he enlisted and found that the Navy thought blue meant black. Squids. Shiny gray hat pulled down over long brown hair. She moved well. Really well. Graceful. She stuck out, actually. She seemed to be dancing down the sidewalk, not just putting one foot in front of the other. From the way she moved, she carried something in her hand. He couldn't see what. Whatever she'd played, he assumed.

Tourn looked above her head and saw the trees of Central Park at the end of the concrete *wadi*. His savior – for her music healed his battered heart in ways he didn't understand – came to the corner. She made the light and struck out across the suddenly un-busy street.

Tourn chewed a lip, conscious of a lot more than usual. Big black men following pretty white girls were in for a world of hurt. Especially if the cops found out. He didn't want anybody to get the wrong idea, especially if that idea lead to pain. Or incarceration.

He felt his side, where he kept his encourager. The crawling fear of living in the dark Down Below had gotten to him a while ago. So he'd found something to help. Two lengths of rusty rebar half again as long as his forearm. Sometime in the unknown past, for some reason, they'd been welded side-by-side. He'd wrapped the bar in wire, and then one end of it in duct tape to make a handle.

It made a handy club.

Holes worn in his big canvas coat made for a handy place to keep it. Out of sight. He'd taken care to grind down the jagged bits, too. He'd seen what happened to people who got scraped up by rusty steel and didn't get seen to.

Those unpleasant thoughts took him up to and across the busy street. He got honked at a couple of times, but that was just the taxis being friendly. Once in the park, he reacquired his mark. Her humming hadn't stopped once, though the song had changed again and again, and it was still as though she walked right behind him.

Only his sense of urgency was stronger. His hands were shaking. His teeth were almost chattering with it. He knew, without knowing how, that she was in deadly danger. Something nearby wanted to do evil to her.

Tourn forced himself to slow down. Running now, scooping her up and carrying her off to someplace safe wouldn't just scare the life out of her. It'd get him in the worst kind of trouble. That was kidnapping, after all.

He blinked, and looked wildly around. The sun slipped below the skyline, leaving the park in deepening shade. His apprehension ratcheted up. Soon, the young woman and her healing music would be in shadow. And he knew what waited in the shadows.

The old fear started to worm its way through Tourney's heart.

He could hear it now, the chittering, chattering susurration of their voices, just on the edge of hearing. They were close, much closer than he liked. And she just walked on, as though she couldn't hear anything.

The musician danced on, moving through the park as though in a dream. She still hummed in his ears, and that helped, but Tourn didn't think she had any clue of the trouble she was walking toward.

He was panting now: from reaction, from adrenaline, from knowing something was coming, but not knowing what. He looked around again, and it dawned on him that they were the only people he could see.

And dark was falling.

Something caught at his foot, and he stumbled off the paved path. His feet slid on the turf and he went down heavily. He'd swear something grabbed his foot and pushed. He rolled over, frenzied limbs flailing, head whipping back and forth. Something in the background noises of the city sounded like children laughing. Children with inhuman mouths, who pulled the limbs off insects to see them squirm.

He saw nothing out of the ordinary. No glowing eyes. No black figures. Central Park at twilight was eerie, devoid of people, though for all he knew, they were no more than a few hundred feet away. Shadows lengthened and deepened as the night closed its grip on the city. What should have been a peaceful, daily transition now pulsed with juddering menace.

The humming stopped.

Frantic now, Tourn heaved himself to his feet. He looked toward where he'd last seen the musician, but saw nothing. No young woman, case in hand, walking down the path. He pulled his encourager out of his coat, gripping it in one sinewy hand, and ran toward where he'd last seen her.

The humming had stopped, and he didn't know where she had gone.

Chest heaving, Tourney skidded to a stop on the spot where she'd been and whipped his gaze around.

There!

In the shadows under a footbridge a knot of figures struggled. What light there was gleamed on the musician's pale face. And in her angry eyes. A bunch of the creatures from Down Below surged out of the shadows. One of them latched onto her case and pulled.

Tourn's heart froze. Suddenly, he was back in that hot, dusty, deadly street across the world from the city. The musician struggled among black, hairy figures, all claws and glowing eyes, and around them, the ghostly forms of Sergeant Yves and Corp and the others wrestled with demons out of his nightmares. Tourney's mouth went dry and his world contracted to a point. The chittering in his ears was deafening.

The music player shouted angrily and swung a blow at it with her free hand. She connected! There was a flash of golden light and the thing just fell apart with a distant-sounding wail. The light jarred Tourn loose from his frozen reverie.

He wouldn't let it happen again.

All the figures in the shadows under the bridge stood stock still. For a moment only, and then two more of the black creatures pounced, pulling at the case. His songstress screeched and wrapped her other hand around her instrument case. Tourn saw something brilliant and golden tumble from her fingers.

And then he was upon them.

With an explosive grunt, he brought his encourager down on the back of one of the creatures. A hiss burst out of the thing, and it collapsed into a heap. Suddenly a dozen glowing eyes tracked on Tourn. He spun past the surprised girl and drove the end of his weapon into the head of one of the monsters gripping her instrument case.

He felt a crunch, and whatever it was flew into the wall, to slide twitching down it. And then the rest were on him. He swung his encourager and his fist, he kicked and punched, and tried desperately to keep away from their sharp-clawed hands.

They rushed him, piling on top as he fought to stay upright. Though none of them were much bigger than the girl, together they massed much more than Tourney. He sank under their weight, and felt their claws nipping through the layers of cloth he wore to score his sides and back. He flailed, crying out, feeling himself going down.

And then she started to sing.

Words in a language he didn't understand poured over him, lifting his spirits and strengthening his resolve. Her clear, soprano voice seemed to have some effect on the shadow demons, too. Their movements slowed and became jerky, almost reeling.

Tourn got his feet under him again and thrust down with his free hand. Something smooth stuck to his hand as he pushed his way to his feet, and as he struck out with his encourager, it left a trail of brilliant, golden sparks floating in the air.

The creatures shrieked in pain as he pummeled them. Each blow struck one down, some bursting asunder, some collapsing into bubbling heaps. Finally, there were no more left, just melting smears of shadow on the ground.

Tourn stood panting as post-combat reaction set in. It always had for him, and it never took longer than a few heartbeats. Everything shook, and he staggered sideways to lean against the wall. He drew strength from the concrete of his city, and slowly his breathing slowed, his pounding heart calmed.

Finally, he looked up into wide, blue eyes.

She still sang, and he couldn't tell what she was feeling. Anybody who'd just come through what they had, though, was probably pretty tough. He clamped his encourager under his left arm, came to attention, and saluted his savior as her song came to an end.

"Th-th-thank you, m-ma'am." The words always seemed so hard to force out. "Y-y-your s-song saved us. L-l-lance-corporal T-tourney Martin, at your s-s-service." He gulped. It was the longest speech he'd made in months. Maybe years.

"No, Lance-corporal," she said in that same clear voice, "your courage saved my life from the shadows, and for that I am in your debt. I am Melody Devreux, my hero."

Tourney became aware that something was clenched in his left fist. He opened it to see, and beheld a tiny golden coin. Snatches of the battle came back to him. A flash of gold as her fist connected with a monster, trails of sparks as he swung a length of rusty rebar.

"I-I-I th-think this is y-yours, ma'am." He offered her the coin.

Smiling, she gently closed his fingers back around it. She shook her head.

"No, sir knight, I think it should go with you now."

He nodded, feeling the truth of her words in the same way he had known to follow her. Certain, though not knowing why, he knew what to do now.

"I sh-should go."

"And where will you go, Tourney?" He felt concern in her words, but also acceptance.

Tourn gripped the gold coin tightly in his hand.

"I-I-I h-have things I n-need to do, Miss Melody."

She nodded. She tucked something in his pocket. Money, he thought.

"I'll be playing my fiddle in a little park a few blocks away, some days," she said. "I'd like you to come and listen."

He nodded.

"I-I-I h-hope I'll b-be able to, M-miss Melody."

She nodded, her blue eyes shadowed. He thought she knew what he was about.

They walked out from under the bridge, back into the park proper. He noticed the stars were coming out, which was extra strange in the city. As he walked away, he felt Melody's gaze on him.

Tourney Martin ran his fingers along his encourager where it waited patiently under his worn and tattered coat. He felt the edges of the bright little gold coin nestled in his fist, and turned his thoughts to Down Below.

He had some shadows to see to.

HEAL THYSELF

THE BACK OF MICHAEL RUNEY'S FAVORITE HEAD BOUNCED OFF OF Cinder Bella's bar on the way down. His vision vanished in the expected flash of light, customary when he took a blow to the head. After nearly a decade as a bouncer in the city, he'd gotten used to that. A few nights off and the contents of the economy-size bottle of aspirin in his medicine cabinet saw him through the worst of the headaches.

This time, though, the blinding flash brought a friend.

Mike - people, especially drunk people, seemed to like calling him Mickey, on account of his last name, ha ha - floated in an ocean of non-sound. It went right at home with his non-sight. Except.

He'd floated in the actual ocean a few times. He'd been down to the Shore in August once - got in a nice little fight there, too - and spent a chunk of time just floating on his back. The warm water held him up, and the summer sun beat gently down. With the sea in his ears, he felt so relaxed, so at home that he nearly fell asleep.

This wasn't like that at all. Right at the edge of hearing, a rushing, roaring murmur tried to tell him the secrets of the universe. He was dead certain that if he listened too hard, he'd scream his lungs out.

He came too just in time to see a leg – covered in fishnets and stuffed in a size thirteen, pointy-toed, patent leather boot – swing back. Spilled booze, most of it fruity and cloying, sent fumes up his nostrils from the floor just a few inches away. Mike rolled sideways into the other leg just as the toe swung toward his ribs. Applying just the right amount of violence, he grabbed, twisted and pushed upward with an explosive grunt.

There were downsides to bouncing at one of the most notorious gay bars in the West Village, but all out brawls usually weren't one of 'em.

The big queen went over backward - a definite con to wearing five-inch stilettos, Mike thought - creating just enough space to get to one knee. His thick, leather bike jacket soaked up a couple of blows as he got to his feet. He left the armor pads in for just such occasions. He mostly let 'em come in, as it wasn't his job to hurt people.

He'd learned that one early, to his shame.

Finally on his feet, Mike set his back to the bar and defended his territory. Mostly, as usual, this involved whipping elbows at all comers and keeping an eye out for the rest of Bella's tough guys. Bella - Frank to his friends, or while off the clock - hired big men to see to the smooth operation of his establishment. Mike saw Gerald and Tomás headed in from the door.

Nancy and Virginia - Bella hired some tough girls, too - were spraying the brawl with soda water from behind the bar again. Each gripped an empty in her offhand and smacked the hell out of anybody stupid enough to get that close. Assuming he survived this one, he'd have to talk to them about that. He didn't want either left holding a handful of broken glass. Or handcuffed in the back of a cruiser, as bottles could be lethal. They didn't break nicely like you see in the movies.

Mike felt the melee starting to cool off, when a bantam-weight little bruiser flew at him out of the press. The kid's eyes glared madness and his mouth hung open in a rictus snarl. His white net tank top did little to hide the nut's impressive muscle definition. Light from the spots flashed off knuckles more or less encased in shiny metal rings.

Mike felt a moment's wave of unease. The guy coming at him wasn't going to give up short of a knock out: he'd seen enough fights and fighters to sense it. Mike's gaze zeroed in on what he thought at first was a weird necklace. It hung around the crazed attacker's neck, and looked made out of hard black metal and animal parts.

And then it moved.

Dried-up, leathery-looking tentacles slid across the kid's chest, and twined around his neck. Spiny bits that could have done for spider legs - if they'd come off a black widow as big as a hubcap - pricked at the kid's ribcage. Mike thought he saw blood running down the boy's torso. Plates that might have been metal, or might have been something far more insectile rustled and shivered as the kid moved into Mike's range.

But Mike couldn't move.

The big bouncer felt like somebody just poured ice into his veins. Muscles accustomed to obeying commands instantly lay frozen and locked. It was all Mike could do to stand as the little man with the crazy eyes and the terrifying thing raged into him.

Armored fists thudded into Mike's torso. Each blow felt like his attacker wielded hammers. Mike had gone up against drunks and junkies with less strength. He tried to defend himself, but couldn't so much as lift his arms.

Despair rose, threatening to swallow him whole. The kid cackled, and the pace of his blows increased. Mike sagged, and a punch glanced off his forehead. He felt heat as blood sheeted down his face, and the world flashed white again. Instead of the sea, though, Mike saw the crazy kid's disturbing collar thing.

But in the space inside his head, the tentacles weren't dried and leathery. Slime coated leprous-pale flesh writhed against the non-background, and chitinous legs the bright shiny crimson of a hooker's lips scrabbled and twitched, trying to bring the thing closer to Mike.

To his face.

A surge of primal horror swept Mike down. The last thing he saw as his vision cleared and returned to the world around him was a pinpoint of horrified despair deep in the kid's eyes. Then Mike saw nothing at all.

†††

Mike's eyes flew open and his big, scarred hands closed vise-like on the wrists of the paramedic hovering over him. For a moment before he realized where he was, Mike's vision was still filled with lashing, twisting, snapping tentacles springing from a mass of slime and horn-slick ruby shell, chasing him through the dark corners of his soul.

"Ahh!" The rather attractive paramedic cried out, black eyes wide in her suddenly pale face. Mike's crushing hands sprang off her wrists as though he'd grabbed red-hot metal bars instead of human flesh and bone. The skin on her face returned from ashen to a more normal healthy dark olive color.

"S-sorry." Mike blinked his eyes rapidly, trying to figure out where he was. Cinder Bella's still, judging by the ceiling, snaky with hung cables for the PA, stage and mood lighting. The overheads glared down into eyes made sensitive by unconsciousness. He took it all in while trying to rid himself of the hideous dream images.

"Where'd the little guy with the creepy necklace go?" Mike asked, still trying to come to grips with what he'd seen in the last moments of the brawl. As his shuddering heartbeat slowly calmed, Mike pushed himself up to his elbow and looked around. Bella's looked like there'd been a battle in it, which made sense. Tables and chairs were knocked all over, and more than one other EMT crouched over a prone figure. Bella - Frank - sat on the bar, talking to a cop. Another officer leaned against the front door.

Mike craned his head around, ignoring the paramedic's sharp warning not to move as she applied temporary sutures to the cut on his forehead. He was struck by how her gentle hands didn't hurt. Then his heart sank: other cops covered the rest of the exits, including the trapdoor behind the bar from when the place had been the entrance to a speakeasy.

Somebody must have died.

Dammit. He was going to lose his job over this one. As the head bouncer, he was answerable for a lot of what went down in a fight. If they were lucky, he'd be the only one fired. He shook his head - angry at himself and ashamed for only then thinking about the poor, presumably, dead person - and immediately wished he hadn't.

"I know you're tough, Mr. Runey, but stop moving your head," the pretty EMT told him, her beautiful eyes crackling now with anger. "Dennis - at the door - said he saw you go down twice during the fight. How you don't have a split skull I can't imagine, but you'll have a nasty headache for a while, regardless." Throughout the rant, her hands never stopped moving. She closed up the gash on his head, cleaned up his face and helped him pick the glass out of the back of his jacket.

"Ma always said my skull was made of rock," he muttered, and saw what looked suspiciously like a smile dance around her lips. He hadn't been smiled at by a pretty girl in a while.

"Thank you, Miss-" Mike left it open, hoping she'd tell him her name.

She smiled. Right out in the open, this time.

"Pahlavi. Yasmin Pahlavi. You're welcome, Mr. Runey, but let's not meet like this again." She had a dimple in her left cheek.

"Call me Mike."

She smiled again, and pushed a few strand of her straight, black hair out of her face. Mike's heart started to pound again, though not from fear. He opened his mouth to ask for her number - hey, it could happen - when a voice completely derailed his train of thought.

"Mickey Runey?" He really didn't like people calling him that, especially not someone like this. The voice in question spoke the with the clipped tones of officialdom: all I'm-supposed-to-be-here-and-I-don't-want-to-have-to-make-your-life-a-mess-really, and that's-an-awfully-nice-life-you're-living-there-shame-if-something-happened-to-it. He distrusted those tones on an instinctive level. Lower-level bureaucrats always wanted to make somebody else's life harder. As far as Mike was concerned, it came of being a bureaucrat.

This one looked like most of the rest he'd ever dealt with. Middling height, middle build, just starting to slide to fat as time in a chair caught up to him. Slightly shaggy haircut, cheap off-the-rack suit, glasses frames straight out of the 1960s. Perfectly standard bureau-bum, but for the hint of something shiny where his shirt gapped over his chest.

Mike shrugged and stayed where he was, lying on the floor. He found that officials preferred talking to people from positions of power. So long as he didn't stand up and tower over the suit by a good head, he figured he'd be fine. Also, not giving up much in the way of information.

"Mr. Runey, I'm Sergeant Timmons, NYPD," the man pulled a badge out of his jacket and held it at Mike's eye-level. His tone probed, as Mike expected. Cops always wanted to use your own words to trip you up. "Several eyewitness have you knocking over a, ah, Ms. Cherry Jubilee, and then assaulting an unnamed man."

Mike shrugged when the guy paused. He hadn't known the big queen's name, and it looked like the cop still didn't, if all he had was her nom de guerre. So to speak.

The cop frowned.

"Mr. Runey, I'd really appreciate it if you helped me out here." There it was, the we're all friends here tone. Mike had heard that one a lot, too.

"Well, Sergeant Timmons, you haven't asked me any questions yet." Out of the corner of his eye, Mike saw Yasmin's lips twitch.

For a bare moment, Sgt. Timmons stared down at Mike. The light from the fluorescents overhead hit the cop's glasses just right, completely hiding his eyes behind artificial glare. Somehow, it seemed to Mike as though the room had darkened. His pulse sped up at the shaded hint of danger.

"Of course." And now the cop's tone was guarded. "What do you remember of the brawl?"

Mike frowned. He'd been holding up one end of the bar, when suddenly everybody seemed to start throwing punches. He filled in Sgt. Timmons on what he remembered, carefully omitting references to his nightmarish dreams. And while he mentioned the creepy kid's creepier necklace, Mike chose not to mention how it seemed to reach for him right at the end.

By the time Mike finished recalling the evening to the cop, Yasmin finished with him and moved on to somebody else across the room. Sgt. Timmons or no Sgt. Timmons, Mike was pretty sure he had a chance with her, and wanted to finish this up quick. Before she left.

The cop frowned at him again.

"Mr. Runey, you claim to have no memory from the time your assailant came out of the crowd and attacked you until the point where you awoke while Ms. Pahlavi treated you."

Mike nodded. Safer than quibbling with the cop's choice of words. And accurate enough, in its own way.

"So you also claim you don't remember kicking your unnamed assailant in the chest, and sending him flying halfway across the room?" Skepticism lurked in the back of Sgt. Timmons voice. The trick was in the words, though.

"Frank's gotta have tapes," Mike said, jerking a thumb at a shiny, black bulb tucked over the bar. "I guess those should have what you're looking for." Answering the question in his usual direct manner would probably have gotten Mike in trouble. Have you stopped beating your wife yet?

Something about Timmons creeped him out. Beyond the whole cop thing. After a moment, it came to Mike. It was as though his body was trying to say things his mouth wasn't. Looking a little closer - casually, casually, it wouldn't do to piss off the good sergeant - he noticed dark stains at the detective's pits and at his neck.

Which was a little weird. The cop wasn't that big a man. He wasn't even fat. Just a little chunky. Certainly no bigger than Mike was, himself. And the suit, while wool, shouldn't have been enough to make him sweat like that. Mike found the room just a bit chilly without the usual crowd of gyrating club-goers.

"So you don't remember kicking a kid half your size across the room?" The overhead light still reflected off Timmons's glasses, hiding his eyes behind them.

Mike felt his eyes narrow, and forced his face into stillness.

"Like I told you, Sergeant, this guy - not a regular - came out of the crowd at me. He looked hopped up on something, and for whatever reason, I blacked out." Smooth and easy did it. Mike had nothing to be angry about. Bar fights weren't common, but weren't anything to freak about, either. On the other hand, the coppery smell of spilled blood and the sour odor of spilled booze set Mike's guts to roiling. The questioning didn't help any. "The first thing I remember after that was waking up with Ms. Pahlavi working on me."

Timmons's lips twisted - ever so slightly - as though he tasted something he didn't like. The skin just over his eyebrows tensed.

Same for the skin over his cheekbones. Mike noticed the fingers of his right hand twitching, and wondered if the good officer wasn't maybe on some kind of substance, as well.

He wanted something. All cops did - hell, everybody did - but Timmons wanted something specific. Something he wasn't getting. Taking in the cop's almost labored breathing, Mike realized that the smaller man gave off the same tells as a guy looking for a fight. His pulse pounded in response.

Deliberately, he leaned back on his elbows. He hated leaving himself open to a guy that seemed like he might snap, but he could probably sweep the cop's legs if it came to it. More than that, though, he looked far less threatening this way. Getting attacked by a cop in the city could easily turn into having attacked the cop in the first place.

"Sergeant, are you feeling okay?"

The cop started, his whole body spasming. For a moment, Mike thought Timmons would fall over, but he caught himself.

"Wha-? Yes, yes I'm-" His words cut off abruptly as a wet, tearing cough ripped through his chest. "I'm-" Another cough sounded as though Timmons's ribs had broken and were trying to shred their way out of his torso. The sergeant splayed his feet against the spasms shuddering through his body, and his free hand - the shaking right hand - dipped into a pocket. It emerged with a white handkerchief.

Timmons pressed the cloth to his mouth, stifling the sound - if not the violence - of his convulsions. Mike's scalp tightened on his skull as the detective bent over. The cop's shirt front writhed as he jerked from the deep, tearing coughs. Nobody else in the room could see: Mike had the best seat in the house. So to speak.

Timmons's tie dangled and twitched in time with his shuddering. As it bounced aside, Mike caught flashes of whatever it was on the cop's chest reflecting the shine of the club's lights.

Something black, shiny and twitching. Inky froth stained the white handkerchief and the sergeant's lips. Mike's stomach clenched so tight he fought the sudden urge to vomit.

Suddenly, the door to the back burst open with a bang. Mike cranked his head around. He saw a tall homeless man with skin nearly as dark as the leather of Mike's jacket. His face was seamed with scars, for all he wasn't that old. In one hand he gripped a length of metal as though it was some kind of sword. He scowled, and his eyes seemed to glow in his face, though with what emotion Mike couldn't tell. That fiery gaze roamed over the club, pausing briefly on Mike. An eyebrow quirked up, and then his attention snapped to Timmons. He raised his club and pointed it at the stricken cop.

"You!"

Without a word, Timmons spun on his heel and staggered toward the door. Crouched half over, cloth still pressed to his mouth, the cop straight-armed the club's heavy door. A muffled squawk sounded as he went through.

With a muttered curse, the bum made to follow. His first step into the club, however, his foot came down on an overlooked bottle. The bottle slid out from under his foot, and caromed off a succession of chairs before somehow coming to rest standing upright.

At the same time, the bum's foot went out from under him, sending him headlong to the floor. With a strangled grunt, he managed to get his hands under him on the way down. As he hit, a shiny bit of something flew out from under him.

It skipped off the floor and flew right at Mike's head. He whipped a hand up and felt something smack into his palm, just as the homeless guy lunged off the floor with an explosive grunt. Mike felt the man's glare as if it was a summer sunlight on his skin. He was astonished to see the man cock his head and then wink at him. Then the man moved so quickly he seemed to teleport through the front door.

Mike found himself on his feet, following Timmons and the nameless bum without a conscious decision. He vaulted an upturned chair, and ignored both the twinges from his ribs and Frank's angry yell from the stairs up to the offices. He was probably fired, anyway. And if he still had a job, he wouldn't lose it over that, so what did it matter? Mike slowed at the door, cracking it just enough to get outside. He was mindful of the cry he'd heard, and didn't want to duplicate it.

He needn't have bothered. Aside from scattered medical supplies, there wasn't anybody on the other side of the door except for a growing crowd of skimpily-dressed club-goers huddled together against the evening chill. He singled out one slimly androgynous form clad in black leather leggings and a shimmering pink top.

"Hey, the guy who just ran through here: where'd he go?"

A dozen voices babbled a dozen different responses, and Mike felt his face slide into what he thought of as his Don't Mess With Me Right Now mask. Amused grass-green eyes locked gazes with his own brown orbs.

Mike swept his arm across his body in a cutting gesture. Combined with the angry-face the chatter died, cut off cold.

"Not everybody," he pointed at his chosen source, "just you."

"Mikey, sweetheart, is Bella's open?" The voice of smokey honey combined with the distinctive eyes snapped Mike's growing ill-temper like the proverbial twig. Only one person besides his mother called him "Mikey."

"Anne?" Anne Cavanaugh was one of the few people at the center where Mike trained who could keep up with him, big bruiser that he was. And big as he was, Anne was lightning chained in human form. She couldn't take him, but he had a hell of a time catching her at all. "Guy in a suit followed by a tall homeless guy with a club: which way?"

Mike watched the humor lurking in Anne's eyes fade as she caught the tension suffusing his frame. She jerked a thumb to one side, pointing to his left.

"Female EMT took off after 'em," Anne informed him. "Need backup?"

But Mike was already moving.

As soon as he heard Yasmin had followed the bizarre duo, Mike spun and ran. His long legs ate up the pavement as he dodged and juked around passersby. Fortunately, foot traffic was lighter this late at night. That and most people get out of the way of a big white bouncer moving at speed. Especially when he's wearing a "get out of my way" expression.

A couple walking arm in arm split to either side of Mike as he went through. To reveal an older woman bent over something on the sidewalk. Strangling a curse, Mike skidded to a stop, just short of bowling her over.

"I think that man is very ill," she told the world at large. Her voice quavered but Mike could see a glint of something undefinable in her bright eyes. She pointed at her feet, drawing Mike's gaze downward.

A wadded white handkerchief lay crumpled on the sidewalk. The cloth huddled forlorn in a shiny mess of viscous fluid. Some of which was the inky, oily black Mike expected to see once he recognized Timmons's rag. Some of the fluid was a milky pearlescent. For all it was one pool of yuck, the two colors didn't mix.

Mike looked into the old woman's curious gaze.

"Which way?" he asked.

They stood at the entrance to a shadowed alley. Mike couldn't tell how far it went, or even what it contained. The woman pointed down it with one crooked finger.

"I hope that girl can help him," the old woman said as Mike walked into the dark alley.

A feeling of strangeness - of some menacing other - drifted on the night air. As he stalked down the alleyway, Mike questioned his purpose. A weird - and creepy, and maybe dangerous - cop ran off. A weird - and scary, and very dangerous - homeless guy chased after him. Then Yasmin took off after them both. And she was a paramedic: young, female and not scary at all that he was aware of. And he still hadn't asked her out.

Mike took some heart from that as he crept through the dark. The other two could go hang, as far as Mike was concerned. Especially Sergeant Timmons, NYPD, he of the persistently accusatory questions.

The buildings around him walled out the noises of the city, weirdly distorting the sounds that meant normal to Mike. A siren in the distance became the cry of some great hunting beast. The rumble of vehicles, above and below the street both, morphed into the shuddering function of some monstrous digestion. And the ever-present chatter of humanity took on the ominous, skittering tones of the distant voices he'd tried not to hear earlier in the evening, while unconscious on the bar floor.

Mike shivered.

The bite of a fall night in the city crawled inside his jacket and raised goosebumps on his bare scalp, slick now with sweat. He rubbed his free hand over it and made a note to shave sometime soon. Assuming "soon" ever came.

Mike heard the quiet sounds of a struggle from somewhere ahead of him. A grunt, the scuff of feet, a muffled clang, and sounds he couldn't identify drifted to his ears. Mike picked up his pace, and saw dim light in front of him. Despite the risk, he broke into a run when he heard an anguished cry cut off by the dull thud of flesh hitting cement.

Mike came into an open loading area, dimly lit by a dull and faded security bulb. What he saw froze his marrow and locked his muscles tight. Mike skidded to a stop and went down on one knee very nearly right next to Timmons. Who barely looked human anymore.

Mike's stomach rebelled, but his throat was clamped too tightly shut to vomit – though he so desperately wanted to.

Timmons squatted on bandy legs, arms hanging limp at his sides. His head was thrown back, and the light of the dim bulb shone on his glasses. His shirt hung in tatters from his shoulders. Rising out of the ruin of his suit, clawing and writhing and grasping at the air rose the same sanity-shredding mass of tentacles and spines Mike had seen in his nightmares.

Infinitely worse than that, however, was the bulbous protuberance that forced the cop's jaws wide. An arm-thick column of muscle studded with spine-like hairs writhed more than two feet out of Timmons throat. Shiny with slime, the abomination culminated in an orifice that could only be called a maw. Fangs the green-brown of tobacco juice set in a shapeless, eyeless bag of naked muscle clashed together with a sound that froze Mike's guts.

The bum leaned against the wall, just under the light. He favored his left side, and from his heavy breathing and the lines carved into his face, Mike knew he was in serious pain. He held his odd club out in front of him like a shield. The dim light set the edge of the metal bar on fire, and it seemed to glow with a clean, golden light of its own.

The thing that rose from Timmons open mouth ceased its gnashing and turned toward Mike. It gave off waves of malevolent curiosity that he did not like in the least. And then, in a voice that took Mike back to a sea of mind-rending utterances, it spoke.

"Tch-tch-tch, ah. Krkrkrtcha, come, meat and join us." The stridulating, sibilant words were barely understandable, and at the same time horribly, horribly clear. "You shall make us a strong, new host." To Mike's horror, the muscular stalk stretched toward him, turning the once-human body with it.

Mike, still on one knee, cried out in disgust and fear as the hideous thing shambled toward him. In reflex, he thrust his hand out in front of him, and did something he hadn't done in his adult life.

Mike prayed.

Heat flashed through his hand, and a brilliant gold glare banished the night. The un-Timmons jerked away and screamed, a shrill, thin shriek that bounced off the walls around them and bored into Mike's head.

In that moment, the bum leaped away from the wall that supported him. With a shout, he took a long step and brought his club sweeping down. The bar left a trail of shimmering phosphorescence as it sped toward its target. Instead of bludgeoning the monstrosity, however, it cut cleanly - almost effortlessly - through that dark, fleshy column.

The thing's scream cut off as its maw fell. Mike saw the horrible mouth hit the pavement... and splash, going from solid flesh one second to inky, stinking fluid upon impact. Likewise, the column of its neck and the mass on Timmons's chest melted into gelatinous slime. Timmons himself fell to his knees, coughed and vomited that same odd mixture of inky slime and pale fluid. He sighed once and slumped over on his side, apparently unconscious.

Mike blinked, trying to make sense of what he'd just witnessed.

The bu- no, the fearsome street warrior walked over to Timmons, taking care not to step in the puddle of ichorous goo. He nudged the fallen cop with one foot. The effort proved too much, and he staggered several steps to fetch up against a dumpster.

Mike got to his feet and started over to him, but the warrior shook his head and pointed across the clearing. A boneless mound, clad in a paramedic's uniform, lay collapsed against the building, huddled just inside a door. Mike's heart rose into his throat.

"Take c-c-care of the g-girl first."

Yasmin lay in a heap against one wall. An arm-full of medical gear lay scattered about her. He dropped to his knees, unsure what to do. She was unconscious - to have lain unmoving through that episode, she'd have had to be - slumped on her side, in an almost fetal curl. A rising bruise - crowned with a split over her cheekbone - marred most of the exposed side of her face. Even as forceful as that blow must have been, it couldn't be what knocked her out. He knew he wasn't supposed to move someone with a possible head or neck injury, but he hadn't even seen what happened.

Mike's fingers itched. Absently, he scrubbed them on his jacket, and thought furiously. The itching grew to a fierce tingling, as though thousands of tiny bees buzzed just under his skin. Distantly he realized he held something in his other hand, something he'd thrust at the Timmons-monster. Something that resonated with the tingling in his fingers.

Mike glanced at his other hand, fingers clenched tight around-clenched around what? Whatever it was had both hands tingling now. He uncurled his fingers to reveal a small gold coin, shining in the palm of his hand. Dim light from the single security lamp hit the coin and flashed golden brilliance into his eyes.

The world blurred.

Everything but the coin: that was clear and crisp to his sight. Mike's pulse thundered in his ears, in the cavity between them. His pulse slowed, and boomed in the cavernous place he now seemed to inhabit. BOOM, the hollow sound rang, and a net of crazed red lines sprang up in his vision. BOOM, and they pulsed, now bright, now dim, against a darker red background. BOOM, and that same brilliant golden light flared in the middle of the net.

Mike realized he was staring at his hand. Not the skin, as he was used to it, roughened and scarred by years of hard work, both in and out of the gym. No, the vessels and muscles that lay under that workaday skin of his. He saw scar tissue where he'd cut his finger real deep as a kid, the broken or dislocated joints he'd suffered before he'd learned not to hit people in the head.

The coin flashed again, filling Mike's vision with gold, blinding him.

When he could see again, Mike looked at Yasmin. Her face was still there: the same olive skin, the same eyes shut tight with pain, the same mark on her cheek now deepening to an ugly purple in the dim light, with a thread of vivid crimson tracking down her face. Under it all, though, he saw her tissues. Her blood flashed in pulses timed with her heartbeat.

Unthinking, Mike rubbed the thumb of his hand over the bruise on her face. His other hand - the one holding the coin - slid around to cup the back of her head. Obeying some prompt he didn't understand, and wasn't even fully conscious of, and without moving a muscle, Mike pushed.

He gasped as his heart stuttered in his chest. His pulse raced to match time with Yasmin's, and all his muscles clenched at once. Physically, it was like when he went for a max weight lift at the gym, like he threw everything he had into one punch. Every muscle fired at once, driving toward a single goal.

Emotionally it was very, very different. Everything fell away: the smells of the street, the sounds of the city at night, the feel of Yasmin's skin and hair. All was stillness but for pure will, driving toward that same singular goal.

And like that, it was over.

Mike rocked back on his heels, drained. He looked around, gaze wandering, taking in everything, but seeing very little. The nameless warrior stood just to one side, watching Mike with an unblinking stare. Not a little disconcerting, actually.

"Mr. Runey?" Yasmin stared up at Mike, her dark eyes lustrous in the half light. Confusion and just a bit of fear filled her voice. Mike realized with a start that her head still rested in his hand. She looked much smaller now than she had when he'd been the one on the floor. "What are you doing here?"

"W-w-what d-do you remember?" The warrior asked, his voice as intent as his expression.

Yasmin lifted one hand and ran it over the back of her head. Her fingers stilled when they met Mike's. Her questioning gaze probed deep into his.

"I remember Sergeant Timmons bursting through the door. I remember he looked sweaty and feverish, all hunched over. I remember chasing after him, yelling at him to let me help him. And then-" She paled, her face shadowing with remembered horror. "Oh, God. That, that thing came out of his mouth and he tore his shirt off and there were more things on his chest." She closed her eyes and shuddered. "And then he hit me, and I blacked out."

"How do you feel?" Mike asked, his voice rough with sympathy.

"Good. Very good, actually."

"Do you hurt anywhere?"

"No." The word was music to Mike's ears. He was sure she should have a concussion from impacting the wall. At least, maybe serious skull damage. "I should, but I don't. Why is that?"

"Him," the warrior pointed at Mike. Wonder suffused his voice. "H-he's a healer."

Mike knew it was true, though he didn't understand it in the least.

"And, if y-you can m-manage it again," the warrior said with a wry smile that twisted the scars on his face, "I'd appreciate it if y-you c-could d-d-do it for m-me."

It was easier the second time. Not easier, actually, just faster. Or maybe just more familiar. After Mike saw to the warrior, who introduced himself as Tourney, he took care of Timmons for good measure.

Or tried to, at least. In what he was coming to think of as heal-vision, Mike saw a grayish shadow in the sergeant's chest. And a darker one in his head. Mike couldn't do anything about them, as there didn't seem to be anything physical about them. When he said so, Tourney nodded.

"W-what I thought: the shadow-beasts rode him hard."

He explained a little of his experiences fighting monsters under the city. Yasmin, who'd gotten to her feet while Mike tried to heal the cop, shook her head.

"I don't know how in the world I'm going to write the report for tonight."

"D-don't. It won't help. G-go to the park near the Flatiron Building tomorrow. Late afternoon. T-t-together. Listen to the f-f-f-" Their savior scowled. "Violinist. Watch the crowd." He stared down at the comatose policeman for a brief moment. "If he recovers, take him, too."

The tall warrior turned and started walking into the night. Mike called after him.

"Tourney, what about your coin?" He held up the little gold disc, which obligingly flashed in the dim light.

"Hold onto it, for now, M-mike. You'll know when it's time for it to move on, " he said as he stepped into the darkness. Just barely visible in the shadows, he stopped and turned. He smiled, eyes and teeth glowing. He spun his odd club around his hand. Mike's scalp tightened as the metal bar left flickering golden streaks in the darkness. "Me, I've learned a couple things."

Yasmin turned to stare into Mike's eyes. Both their mouths hung wide open. Hers was the first to close.

"Well, you heal people," she brushed fingertips across a cheek absent of enormous purple bruises, "why shouldn't he be able to make his own light-show?"

Mike nodded, and plucked up his courage for the scariest part of the evening.

"Yasmin, all that healing has worn me out." She turned to look at him, head cocked to one side. "Would you like to come with me and find something to eat?"

BY HANDS AND KNEES

ANNE CAVANAUGH HAD BARELY A HEARTBEAT TO AVOID THE HUGE bruiser's backswing. His knuckles whistling toward her face put her in mind of the aggressive "fangs" of a police cruiser. Big, scarred and politely malevolent. "I'm only now choosing to crush you, but I could have done it all this time. Nothing personal."

Yeah, nothing personal. It wouldn't be personal if the fist connected. And - inconveniently - made a paste of half her face. It might not be much to look at. Just too square of jaw. Just too wide of mouth. Once broken nose. The catalog went on, but her attention didn't. Suffice to say, Anne's face verged on striking without quite hitting beautiful. But it was hers, and no bastard was going to mess it up. Even if he was two-fifty of solid beat-down.

Anne slid her point of balance back a fraction of an inch, and the fist brushed just past her face. She felt it catch at a few of the hairs - electric blue this week - that'd escaped her headband during the struggle.

The thuggish face carved itself into a scowl. A deeper scowl, really.

Mike always scowled while he fought. Anne had always thought it was kind of cute, really.

Sliding back that necessary fraction of an inch put her weight over her back foot, so she snapped the other in a low kick at Mike's groin. He took it on his thigh, and Anne was glad she used proper form. She didn't enjoy kicking rocks at all, and preferred to wear nothing lighter than steel-toed boots when she had to.

Mike threw a jab toward her chest. If it connected, the punch would drive Anne off balance, perhaps even land her on her back on the mat. So she didn't let it land. Anne rolled around that big, scarred fist. She tapped him on the underside of his wrist as it went past, hard enough to throw him off balance instead. A little footwork, a solid strike to the floating ribs, and the touch - and match - would be hers.

Anne floated sideways and planted her feet, rotating her hips to bring the strength of solid grounding into her strike. Mike was going to feel this one, side of beef though he might be. She twisted, rotating from her pelvis through her spine and her shoulder, and finally out her right arm in a textbook blow.

Right into the meat outside his interposed elbow. One moment, Mike's arm was extended out in front of him; the next it guarded his ribs, and her punch did precisely nothing.

She'd had him: she'd been certain of it. And in that moment of fouled certain, Mike struck back. He pivoted, grounded his foot just behind hers and spun. His spine uncoiled, and Anne flew through the air.

She had a brief view of the mirrors lining one side of the studio, albeit upside down. Shelley's horrified face - again, upside down - flew by. Anne's little sister still resembled a bit the Ryan she'd been born as. But softened and about a million times more comfortable in herself than Ry had ever been. And then Anne caught sight of Mike's bag where he'd dropped it next to hers.

Suddenly, the bag glowed gold and the world - still upside down - seemed to shimmer. Anne was caught, suspended in a sliver of eternity while everything around her scintillated.

Everything but Chelle and the trio of dark figures in the mirror behind her. They looked human, but were horribly not so. Tall, still - too motionless to be human - the three stood shoulder to broad shoulder, everything shadowed, as though seen through heavily smoked glass.

Three beautiful faces, hard with ancient cruelty, loomed over Anne's oblivious sibling. Enormous eyes of no color Anne could describe rode cheekbones a model would kill for. Straight noses, thin and patrician hung over wide mouths. Mouths almost as wide as Anne's own, though these lips were thin where Anne's had always approached lush.

The world shuddered.

Chelle stared open-mouthed at Anne. One Chelle did, at least. Another Chelle - identical but for the bizarre golden tinge - crouched inside the mirror behind Anne's sister. That Chelle knelt, one hand palm raise to the inside of the mirror and pressed hard against it while the other pounded on the glass. That Chelle stared with wide, horrified, pleading eyes at Anne where she drifted ever so slowly through the air.

The mirror-Chelle mouthed Anne's name as the dark trio unfolded long, black-clad arms. They reached for her, and as one, their lips spread, revealing sharp, even teeth the color of charred bone in dreadful parodies of a human's smile.

Anne's marrow froze. Every muscle of her body tensed, just as time resumed its normal flow. A brief shimmer, and objects regained their colors. The figures in the mirror disappeared, and Anne had a split-second to realize she didn't have time to fall well.

Anne crashed to the floor in a jumble. The mat took the worst of the impact, and for a bare moment, she lay in relative peace. Nothing seemed broken or wrenched beyond the normal pain of taking a landing poorly. Lying still was good. So was breathing, for that matter.

"Annie!" Her sister's voice shattered her brief reprieve from conscious thought.

Anne opened her eyes and beheld Chelle's pale, oval face. Upside down, of course, as seemed to be a pattern recently. The fear in her sister's big brown eyes snapped Anne back into the bizarre vision. Her heart trip-hammered for one painful moment, as she seemed to see the terrible inhuman smiles reaching hungrily for her sister.

Chelle's face was soon joined by Mike's. An expression of confused concern replaced the bruiser's scowl, and then a curiously blank look. It was as though, for a moment, Mike was looking at something totally different without moving a muscle. Then his eyes refocused on hers, and he offered a hand.

"She's all right, Chelle," Anne's friend offered to her sister. The certainty in his voice tripped something in the back of Anne's mind.

How was he so sure she hadn't hurt herself?

She grabbed his hand, and he hoisted her to her feet with an ease that took her breath away. She was shocked - as always - with just how strong her big friend actually was. He always pulled his punches, at least a little. There was something there, something in his past that he'd never told her. She was as sure of that as he seemed to be about her health.

Even as the thoughts flashed through her mind, Avi, their Krav Maga instructor and the nominal owner of the studio poked his mop of curly, blue-black hair out of the office.

"What was up with that, Anne? You haven't taken a fall like that since you started training." He crooked a bushy eyebrow at her. He'd often claimed to be a political refugee from Haifa, but Anne knew for a fact he'd grown up on Staten Island. Avi had a preternatural ability to know when one of his students screwed something up.

"I'm - I'm not sure," Anne said. She was still trying to wrap her head around what she'd seen. Or thought she'd seen. Her stomach muscles quivered with a tension whose source she didn't understand. Well, that wasn't true: she knew where it came from. She just didn't know why she'd seen the vision.

If she wasn't just seeing things. Her disturbing vision happened before she landed, and the fall didn't hurt her head any. She didn't drink anything but water when she and Chelley went clubbing, so hallucinogens were out.

"It-" Mike paused, cocked his head in thought, "-looked like you got distracted."

"It looked like you got overconfident," Chelle piped up.

Anne scowled at her sister, but couldn't argue against the veracity of the supposition. She had gotten overconfident. She hadn't thought so, but the results spoke for themselves. Instead of playing a long game and making Mike tire himself out, she'd gone inside his range for the quick kill. Not good against someone who knew what he was doing.

"Why don't you go a few rounds with the man mountain," Anne growled instead, pride still a bit stung.

"I don't need to: that's what I have you for." Chelle flashed a smile that warmed Anne through. That sweet smile had disappeared for years. Anne said a silent prayer of thanks for Mike, for Avi and for Father Kurt, for men who knew about Chelle's past, and didn't care. Men whose bluff, good nature convinced first Anne, then Chelle that life could be safe again.

"And I have Mike and Avi for when you try to kill me for impudence," Chelle added, sticking her tongue out. She danced away when Anne made a mock grab for her. The little ball on her tongue-stud winked golden in the studio lights.

Instantly, Anne saw her vision, seeing the dark figures reach for Chelle, trapped behind the mirror. It was as though someone had dumped ice-water down her spine. The smile fell off her face and she shuddered. Chelle, still spinning and laughing, missed it. Mike didn't.

"What?" Mike's gaze sharpened.

"Have, have you ever thought you'd seen - something?" Anne asked, picking her words with care. She'd spent more than enough time with shrinks, first getting free of her mother, and then getting Chelle the help she needed, that she was fully aware of what telling the full story of her vision could mean. "Something that seemed, well, impossible?"

It was difficult to tell - for the average person, it would have been impossible - but Anne had been sparring with Mike for the better part of a year. The skin around his eyes and mouth tightened, just a bit. His shorn scalp smoothed down over his skull until it gleamed in the studio lights. His weight shifted slightly forward. Mike was scared. And angry.

For a split second, Anne felt herself mirror his reactions. Just as quickly, she backed off, as she realized Mike hadn't reacted to her. He'd reacted to what she'd said. His expression turned inward, and his eyes went a little glassy. It was a long, long moment before he spoke. In the background, she could hear Chelle joking briefly with Avi, but for Anne it felt like an eternity.

"That doesn't sound as crazy as you'd think, Annie," Mike said. His tone was cautious, full of doubt and - wonder? Her friend kept giving off a strange mix of signals, and it was starting to make Anne's teeth itch. After a thoughtful moment pregnant with unspoken thoughts, Mike opened his mouth.

Chelle took that moment to interrupt.

"Annie!" She bounced away from Avi's office and spun between Anne and Mike. The bundle of excitement was so unlike Ryan's last few tense, fearful years Anne blessed anyone of significance who might be listening. She touched her chest with a fingertip, feeling the outline of the little crucifix that was all the legacy she had of their father. Thank God Chelle wasn't afraid anymore.

"Annie," her sister repeated, bouncing on her toes while her eyes flashed. "Avi said there's a new club down near China Town! It's only been open for a few weeks, and he said it's almost certainly safe! Can we go tonight? Can we? Please?"

A fist seemed to squeeze Annie's heart at Chelle's pleas. She had a hard time denying her sibling anything. In large part because as Ryan, Chelle had experienced a surfeit of hurt and pain. The mere thought of which pricked Anne's eyes with unshed tears, and brought an itchy lightness to her fists that promised a company's misery to any with the wrong idea.

Chelle loved to dance. More, even, than when she'd been Ryan. She was actually comfortable in her own skin, for one. When Ryan said he wanted to join ballet instead of the football team, Daddy had disappeared, damn his flaky eyes. Mother dearest had begun to turn inward, and suckled a canker of bitterness. She'd also insisted on family attendance at a little church. A little backward church, full of small, withered souls.

Which made Chelle's love of mass all the more confusing to Anne, much as she treasured her own meager faith. Father Kurt's truly unconditional love soothed both their souls.

Anne had always encourage her sibling's love of dance. She saw it much the same as her own need to practice here in the studio. To that end, she often accompanied Chelle to clubs. Which was to say, when Chelle went to clubs, so did Anne. Much of the reason was protection: Ryan's boyish prettiness had transformed into Chelle's slim elegance.

Anne looked down into the shining eyes that looked so much like their mother's. If their mother's eyes had ever been that full of joy, neither Anne nor Chelle had ever seen it. It was the light in Chelle's eyes that made her beautiful, though, and Anne wouldn't risk that by letting her wander around the city alone.

"Sure, hon." Chelle's answering squeal brought a warmth to Anne's heart that banished the chill left from her bizarre, dream-like vision.

"Mike, can you come, too?" Chelle spun on her heel and - presumably, as her back was to Anne - implored their big friend. Mike smiled at Chelle, but shook his head.

"Sorry, kiddo; I've got class tonight." Mike was studying for his EMT certification, something of a departure from his usual, more physical, employment. He was still bouncing, but had cut back to make room for his classes.

Also for special tutoring sessions with his new "friend," Yasmin. Anne ground down her jealousy. She wasn't attracted to Mike, exactly. He was good to have around, and Chelle liked him. He was a kind of benevolent older-brother type. The kind Anne had always been too scrawny and female to be.

"Speaking of which, I need to get moving." Mike pulled Chelle in for a quick hug, ignoring her protests of his ickiness, then chucked Anne on the shoulder before moving toward the foyer, where his gear hung near the door.

"Avi," Anne called, eager to get away from her feelings of guilt and inadequacy, old and new. "What's this place called?"

His mop of curly hair shot out the open office door.

"Under Hill."

"Weird name."

Avi's head, the only part of him visible, rocked back and forth.

"Eh. This place used to be called the Island of Many Hills. Don't you know your own history?"

Anne stuck her tongue out at him.

"We only moved here a couple years ago, you big jerk. Chelle and I learned about North Carolina history in school." A place where it hadn't been safe to be as different as they were. As Ryan had been. She strangled the old familiar anxiety with the ease of long practice. People in the big city might care, but not enough to find out. And there were enough oddballs here that they didn't stick out.

"Big jerk, am I?" Avi's bushy eyebrows rose, his face taking on a - completely false - air of hurt innocence verging on indignation. "Big jerk?" His head disappeared, and then reappeared an instant later, bringing with it the rest of his bulk. It always surprised Anne just how short Avi actually was: no taller than Chelle. For all his lack of height, he would easily have made two of Anne's sister. "Just for that, you're going to have to show me you've learned from that fall earlier just why you don't go inside against someone male who out-masses you by half."

Anne groaned over the sound of Chelle's laughter. As Avi brought up his hands, Chelle danced away on quick feet. Anne brought up hands weary from earlier exertion and slowly circled away from her mentor. As Avi moved closer, Anne thought she saw a flash of light through the doorway into the foyer. Then Avi closed and threw a quick jab, and there was no more time for conscious thought or ominous visions, only reaction and training.

†††

Anne rolled her right shoulder as she tried to keep up with her boisterous sister. Again. Hours - and ice packs, as well as a really hot shower - later, and it was still feeling stiff. She suspected it would be for at least a few days.

During their sparring match, Avi had somehow managed to get a grip on her arm. The only way out was a complex - and uncomfortable - twist that had put her arm behind her head, and used the shoulder as a fulcrum to put him off-balance.

He'd reamed her out for using it, and Anne knew she deserved it. It was the kind of trick you could pull in the studio, but would almost certainly get somebody - probably her - seriously injured in a street fight.

Her other hand rested in her jacket pocket, clenched tight around the gold coin she'd found there after practice. The thing was small - just smaller than a dime: she'd checked - but much, much heavier than any other coin she'd ever touched. Heavier than it had any right to be. Anne thought it might be solid gold.

Weird that Mike would just leave it in her pocket. Doubly weird that he'd left no real explanation why. There'd been a note wrapped around it. She'd instantly recognized one of the sticky notes that her friend used for references in his class textbooks. It said, "Just in case - M." And the big lug had only answered her questioning message with, "for luck."

If she didn't know him enough to trust him, Anne would have been pissed. She kind of was, anyway. Better to be angry than confused and fearful. When she'd unwrapped the coin, the light had caught it just right and sent a lance of golden reflection into her eyes. Instantly, all the fear and confusion from her vision had loomed large. Anne didn't know what to do about it, but keep an eye on Chelle. And see that her sister was happy.

A face full of scent jerked Anne's thoughts to a halt, and drove them from her head. Her pulse quickened, and her weight shifted forward over the balls of her feet. She just kept herself from bringing her hands up to cover her core. Smells that shouldn't be in the midst of a downtown lay heavy in her nostrils. On top of the constant sour smell of sumac lay damp moss, leafmold and - she sniffed - tarragon and sage mixed with loam. She smelled trees, as well. And - for some peculiar reason - underlying it all spread a sharp, coppery tang.

Anne looked up from her reverie and saw the door to Under Hill. Twining branches of what looked like living trees wove themselves into a lattice over the entryway. Enormous - for the city - double doors stood wide open. Panels of heavy, age-darkened oak bound in polished metal were studded here and there with what looked to be thick, hand-forged nails. The metal spikes had been hammered through the doors, and the excess length pounded flat to the wood.

An enormous man bulked large in front of one of the doors. Anne was struck by the immediate difference between this bouncer and Mike. Her friend was smaller, for one. A lot smaller, she realized as she got closer. And prettier, by far. This - gentleman - reminded her of a chunk of scarred masonry that had been left in the weather for a couple of centuries.

Small, dark eyes hid under thick, craggy brows. Black, wiry hair stood out from the back of his blocky head in a crest. A broad, flat nose clung to his face over a mouth set in a permanent frown. A mouth that seemed more like an animal's muzzle than anything human. Massive shoulders eliminated any chance he could call the space between his head and his chest a neck. Between the arms that hung nearly to his knees and the black suit transformed him into a caricature of a mafioso.

"G'wan in," he said an abyssal voice. Along with his words, the doorman expelled a cloud of foul-smelling breath that threatened to curl Anne's nose-hairs. She managed to stifle her shudder. Barely. Between the depth of his voice and the stench of his breath, it took Anne a few seconds to realize they'd made it through the front door.

"I expected a longer wait," she muttered to her sister.

Giving no indication she'd even heard, Chelle drifted past her into the - into some kind of antechamber. Anne hurried to catch up. People filled the room, a collection of the young and hopeful. It was an unhip crowd. Or rather, it wasn't a crowd trying to look hip. Anne was surprised to note the crowd was missing the usual mixture of the desperate. Few of the glitterati she'd expected to see. In fact, most of them seemed - from their dress and attitude - artists. Musicians, painters, writers - and dancers.

A spiky thread of unaccounted-for apprehension twisted through Anne's guts. Something felt off. Felt ... weird. Music thrummed on the air. A wild, unbound kind of music, it reminded her of folk music from her childhood. If that music was played by an orchestra full of virtuoso players. And written by a madman.

"Chelle, honey, I'm not sure about-" Anne looked around, and realized her sister had disappeared. Her apprehension ratcheted quickly through concern and into foreboding. A quick scan around told her that while there were plenty of young faces around her, none belonged to her sister.

Anne strangled the nameless dread trying to unfold within. This was a club. A weird one, with a weird doorman, but a club nonetheless. Even if they didn't have a line of hopefuls out the door. Even if they didn't seem to be serving drinks.

Anne took a deep breath and a more careful look around. The room - what she could see of it through the dim light - was made up to look like the inside of - of - of she didn't know what. The industrial concrete floor had been polished until it shone. The walls were covered with some kind of stone facade, and the ceiling! Anne boggled a little at the amount of money it must have taken to make it look like a natural stone cave.

At the far side of the room the floor dropped away. Flickering lights and the way the traffic generally flowed toward the open maw drew Anne. As she neared, she saw a set of stairs descending into a darkness shot through with myriad colors.

In any other club, Anne wouldn't have felt off-balance. Flashing lights and loud music meant dancing. She assumed it was true here, as well. But.

Light the colors of a sun-lit leaves seen through water splashed across steps that looked like they'd been carved of solid marble. Marble the color of healthy flesh. The threads of translucent blue winding through the staircase heightened the discomforting impression.

"The pretty lady should dance." The weird voice - full of strange harmonics - ran a shiver up Anne's spine and sent a jolt of adrenaline through her. An eddy in the crowd revealed the voice's owner. Anne's hand clenched hard around the "lucky" coin Mike slipped into her pocket.

Smooth cheeks swept up from a pointed jaw and framed a sensuous mouth whose full lips bent upward in something that approximated a smile. Prominent cheekbones rode on either side of a straight, puckish nose that flipped up at the end. The owner him - her? no, him - self looked far too young to be in any club, let alone one as new, and therefore exclusive, as Under Hill.

Until she looked him in the eyes.

Old eyes, empty eyes, eyes of no color she'd ever seen. The lights from downstairs flickered in those eyes, giving the lie to the smile on his androgynously beautiful mouth. A cruelty Anne intuited she wasn't supposed to see flared bright in those eyes like uncut gemstones. He nodded toward the downward yawning portal.

"Dance, lady," he repeated. The false smile widened, revealing square, even teeth that Anne utterly failed to trust. That voice - a voice that sounded as though it should have come from multiple throats - betrayed hunger. Hunger Anne was again certain she shouldn't have felt. The press of humanity pushed between them and hid the speaker once again.

It was time and past time to find Chelley and leave. With difficulty, Anne forced herself to relax, and let the flow of mesmerized youth hide the disquieting club owner and draw her down the steps. The smell of damp earth and herbs swirled thickly here, and the coppery scent was a foul taste on the back of her tongue.

The steps descended into a short tunnel that opened into an enormous room made up to look like a cross between a natural cavern and a forest glade. Walls that looked like rough-hewn stone were studded here and there with what seemed to be the boles of enormous trees. Anne looked up and saw the source of the multicolored light she'd seen above.

Globes of brilliant green, blue, yellow and white glowed here and there near what she presumed was the ceiling. The lights shifted through a range of colors and shone through leaves. Enormous leaves - each far larger than her own hand - though otherwise faithful to nature. She recognized oak, maple and alder, among several species for which she had no reference. She couldn't see an actual ceiling for the foliage.

The fortune this place represented set her head spinning. Live musicians clustered here and there, eyes screwed shut, bodies held rigid by the frenzied force of their art. Somehow, they all managed to play together. After a moment of intent focus, Anne realized it wasn't so much that they played together, as their disparate melodies blended perfectly to create that wild, haunting harmony she'd heard above.

A formless unease wrapped itself around Anne's heart. The music was as beautiful as the setting. A part of her longed to throw caution to the wind and embrace the savage magnificence she'd found. She could feel the desire, the yearning toward unlimited freedom Under Hill seemed to represent. To pour out her soul; to give up the pain of life. For a moment, she ached to release her hold on herself and simply become part of the magic.

The guarded, pragmatic steel that had held Anne together when her family had fractured and come apart held her back. Anne ground her teeth, feeling the old anger stirring. She drew back from the metaphysical precipice step by shuddering step. She opened eyes she didn't realize were closed, and happened to look at the face of one of the musicians.

A young man, maybe nineteen or twenty, slim and lanky in the half-starved manner of dedicated musicians stood rooted, caught in the grip of the music. Sweat beaded on his forehead and soaked the black shirt he wore. His fingers blurred on the neck of his violin. Threads of his bow had snapped and whistled through the air as he played, a testament to his fury.

But there was no joy in his face: only slavish concentration. His body strained, pouring forth melody in a torrent, but without a hint of the pleasure he should have evinced. Desperate hunger and something beyond pain etched lines into his face as she watched.

The tiny disc clenched in her fist grew hot, and jumped. Anne's vision shivered, as though all she saw was the rippling surface of a pond. All but the fiddler locked in song before her eyes. She still saw the man as he was, but strangely laid over - or just inside - his features, Anne saw a ghostly, ethereal copy of him. The replica moved just out of time with the physical reality, and pulsed rapidly in a beat that mirrored his racing heart.

Hair, gray and lank, lay matted against a scalp that showed through patches. The lines she saw in his physical face carved even deeper, and multiplied again and again. His already spare frame became a nightmarish, emaciated thing of swollen joints and protruding bones, held together by parchment skin. Even his clothes - grown faded, threadbare and moth-eaten - reflected the transformation.

Anne blinked, and tried to swallow through the new-made desert of her throat. The brief vision ended, but Anne could now see the cracks in the grotto. Nothing physical: the club still seemed carved out of living rock and monstrous trees. She saw through whatever magic kept the musicians in harmony, whatever parasitic force lured the young and creative into Under Hill. And proceeded to suck them dry.

With fresh eyes, Anne saw the fiddler's frenetic motion betrayed exhaustion. She was certain he would eventually collapse, alive perhaps, but drained of everything that made him more than a sack of meat. And she had no idea how to stop it, or even if she could.

Anne's eyes widened as she looked around. It wasn't just the musicians. Her stomach roiled as she realized that those who didn't play danced, moving together in swaying, twitching rhythm. Bare heartbeats earlier, it would have been beautiful - in a way, it still was - but now, Anne was disgusted by the impressions she received. Glazed eyes stared at nothing, limbs wove through each other while torsos bent, slid over and across each other. As though one mind controlled them all, moved them as one.

But not perfectly.

The same flaws - if they weren't completely intentional - affected the dancers as well. At random, an arm twitched out of alignment here. There, a foot miss-stepped. The whole corrected quickly enough, but if you paid attention, you could see the cracks in the facade. If a single mind did guide the movements of all of the erstwhile agents, it had some kind of palsy.

And over it all, Anne still tasted copper and forest.

"Dance, pretty lady."

Anne understood now why the - no appropriate word came to Anne for the strange, androgynous person who'd spoken to her above - polytonal voice sounded so wrong. The words issued from the dozen or so closest throats. Those glazed eyes, staring at some other world, turned as one to her. Jaws moved, lips curled in dread-inducing parodies of human smiles.

"Dance with us."

It was the same voice. Anne's gorge rose as she felt her feet trying to obey and move in rhythm to the music. Horror and rage fought for dominance, rooting Anne to the spot. Part of her desperately wanted to flee, to disappear. Another part - an intransigent, rocky part - roared at Anne to push that rictus in.

The coin in her hand grew hot to the point of pain. It jumped in her fist and pulled her around to her left. Anne's feet skidded on the floor, and when she focused on it to regain her balance, Anne's eyes widened. She stood on grass. Green, living grass. A perverse part of her mind suggested that a turf floor probably didn't meet any kind of regulation; the food service inspector alone would have a fit.

An incongruously graceful motion seen from the corner of her eye brought Anne's head up and drew her gaze to some kind of raised platform. Blocks of polished obsidian jutted broodingly from the trampled lawn. Had this been a normal club, she'd have thought it was a dance floor. With the alien strangeness of Under Hill, the thing reminded her of nothing so much as a sullen sacrificial altar.

Upon the polished surface of which floated Chelle. Her sister spun in a slow turn, one leg stretched out behind her, both arms overhead. Anne had seen her perform the same spin any number of times before, but never so slowly. And never with her eyes screwed shut. Chelle was easily fifty yards away, but Anne could clearly see her expression of ferocious concentration. For all the beauty of the motion, fear froze Anne's heart in her chest: Chelle's face bore the same expression as the violinist.

Chelle spun once more, slowly and in time with the music, and then bent backward over her hips. Her outstretched leg swept down and forward and then up in front of her to rest pointing straight up. Her hands planted on the stone surface behind her foot, Shelley's torso straightened, lifting her foot off the floor, coming up into a handstand and splits. Anne was stunned.

She'd seen her sister work - she'd been seeing her dance for years - but never like this.

And then the music swirled into a new, faster tempo. Unseen strings howled, horns blared and drums pounded. It sounded as though some hidden choir had gathered and chanted in unison, just far enough away that Anne couldn't understand the words.

And Chelle exploded into motion. Her legs flashed as she whipped them around and around as though she were some enormous top. And with a twist and a lift, Chelle was back on her feet and whirling about the dais. Now on her hands, now on her feet, occasionally spinning around on her back or head, Chelle's wild dance took Anne's breath away. The beauty of her sister's movements rooted her to the spot, and masked from Anne the desperation in them for a brief moment that felt like an eternity.

And then the coin in her hand flared hot again, sending a spike of genuine pain up Anne's forearm. She tore her fist out of her pocket with a gasp, the pain jerking her gaze away from her sister. Forcing open fingers locked tight from a witch's brew of emotion, Anne stared at the lucky piece in her hand.

The coin glowed with the harsh brilliance of a tiny, golden sun. Further, it spun in place as though someone had driven a nail through its center and into Anne's palm. The pain radiating from the center of her hand felt like someone had done that, as well.

Radiant light blazed up from Anne's open hand, illuminating that part of the crowd nearest her. The glare washed out the soft light from overhead, blasting away at the dusky atmosphere and picking out the lines in the newly gaunt faces. Those closest spun away from the hard incandescence.

Anne's heart thudded against her ribs. Terror for her sister warred with horror at her surroundings, at the sheer alien nature of Under Hill. Both fear and revulsion mixed with a hard fury at whoever sat in the seat of power. Whoever drained brilliant musicians and grace-filled dancers of vitality, reducing them to husks.

Her lips peeled back from her teeth in a feral snarl, Anne started toward where Chelle still danced. Her sister leapt into the air, limbs flaring out as she spun. Chelle landed lightly, collapsing down to one knee and whirling in place on the polished stone like a figure-skater.

As Chelle whirled, Anne stalked forward, her head moving back and forth in small arcs. She was surprised when none of the crowd moved to intercept. Even though the single-minded they did nothing to impede her advance, she could feel the animosity in the air, heavily leavened with amusement. Anger uncoiled in her breast, and galvanized her into a trot.

When she approached the platform, those three half-glimpsed pools of stillness sprang to horrifying life. The one behind the dais vaulted onto it and, for a moment that turned Anne's stomach, whatever it was that went cloaked in mist and smoke danced with Chelle in a bizarre parody of a tango. The occulted figure and her sister slid from opposite sides, coming together in the center of the stone.

Despite Anne's inability to see it clearly, the thing put what had to be arms around Chelle, and the two - one light, one dark - spun about each other. It was graceful, and it would have been beautiful were it not for her certainty that Chelle was under the control of something alien and wrong and in horrible, terrible danger.

The dancing couple - Anne's mind cringed away from the word - leapt apart. Chelle sprang backward onto her hands, while the shadowy something came to rest opposite where it started. The other two shadows moved around the corners to flank the primary, all three blocking her path to Chelle.

Bright golden light from the coin in her open palm stilled the swirling shadow that clothed the figures. The smoky mist faded, revealing creatures with human features. Two eyes, nose, mouth, all set in matching expressions of fury and disgust, but completely void of humanity.

Anne froze, shock stealing will from her mind and volition from her limbs. The creatures confronting her - nothing that looked like that could be human, at least not anymore - were the same ones from her vision in the studio. Right down to the disturbing eyes. In person, Anne could see why she'd been unable to tell their color: the six orbs looking at her from one mind looked to be made things, spheres of some metal polished to a mirror sheen. Those orbs threw back the shifting colors of the cavernous space with a startlingly vivid and painful intensity.

Fear reached up her spine and gripped the base of Anne's skull in fingers that chilled her marrow. She'd been training to fight for years, but she had no illusions: a woman fighting hand-to-hand against most men would lose. Not only were these most men - she didn't know if they even qualified as men despite their appearance - but there were three of them. On top of that, she suspected they'd move as one.

"I was simply going to kill you," one voice - the same voice - issued from three mouths, "but you brought that into my presence. And though you interest me, creature, I will not forgive your transgression." Pallid lips drew back from shiny, black teeth in something closer to rictus than a smile. "I believe I shall make you scream to death before I claim your sibling, and make it like these."

"Chelle?" Anne didn't know why she asked. The creatures' voice spread terror through Her mind was wrapped about in a freezing fog, her muscles turned to ice. Thoughts were hard, like wringing out cloth she couldn't quite get her hands around.

"Chelle." Irony dripped from the word. "Such a creation, and such a dancer. An artist who is also a work of art. The frenzy of creation has claimed your sibling in all possible ways but one, and that one forever out of reach. I felt when you entered my place, thing, that your blood would make an excellent toy of mine."

"Chelle is nobody's toy." Anne forced the words from tongue and lips grown thick and wooden.

"Oh, but it is!" The mind behind the voice sounded proud, as a child presenting a new drawing. "See how it moves, your blood! Full of grace, full of beauty, all that is best of human kine in evidence! And to think it was once as boring as you are, full of nothing but fear and hatred of self. Did you know it still occasionally thinks of itself as Ryan?"

Anne's eyes stung at the cruelty, and she hoped Chelle couldn't hear the words. Chelle had worked so very hard to overcome the pain, to get through the fear. Anne was so proud of her sister, and to hear her beautiful, shining spirit stripped to an "it" hurt, worse even than when their father walked out of their lives forever.

"Your 'Chelle' will dance, will make beauty, until near death, dear, pathetic thing," the voice gloated, "and then these things will bend your precious sibling backward over my altar, pluck out its eyes, and replace them with the silvered orbs of my service. Then Chelle," the voice dripped with revulsion, "will be like these, and I shall find others of your kine kind to consume. Other artists, dancers, singers, wordsmiths and designers, other creators of beauty. Their magnificence and suffering will be delicious!"

The words grated on her mind, and Anne's heart quailed within her. The voice was nearly a physical force, and the music and the crowd mirrored it. When it expressed its hideous joy, the music grew wild and triumphant and the dancers cried out. How could she even fight such a thing?

"But you, thing, aren't even the creation your sibling is." Anne drooped at the disgust flavoring the voice. "You devoted all your time to study, to practice and to protecting your fragile Ryan. You never did anything worthwhile. Not even breed more kine." The voice carried with it the understanding that Anne's very existence was a crime.

Waves of despair swept through Anne. The voice - whoever, whatever it was - spoke the truth. She'd worked hard in school to get the grades to make it into college. She'd done her damnedest to provide once it became clear her parents couldn't, forgoing dance, music and art: anything extra, anything that spent and didn't pay. She'd struggled to graduate with honors, and then worked to afford Chelle's treatments. She'd taken up martial arts, and shooting - though she'd been denied a permit over and over - to have the means to keep Chelle safe. She'd never made anything, done anything that wasn't for the express purpose of helping Chelle. Not for years.

And it hurt. God, it hurt. All Anne's things were really Chelle's things, and she'd never even noticed. She took pride in her skills and in her ability to help her sister achieve her goals. But she hadn't had anything to really call her own for years.

The hard, bright glow from Anne's hand softened into scintillation. The vaporous cloaks swirled up to cover the voice's creatures once again, and the crowd dimmed and faded into the background. But through the sorrow of a life ill-spent, Anne could still see Chelle. Her sister spun into a sequence of kicks, using momentum to switch feet on the fly and turn flips as she went. It was a stunning display, and Anne felt her heart unknot inside her chest at the sheer beauty of it.

"True, I may have put Michelle's needs ahead of my own desires. True, I may have suppressed my own creative drive for my sister. I may not sing, play, or write," Anne said, closing her fingers into fists and shifting her weight, "but I bet I can show you a dance you won't forget."

A tiny, hard kernel in Anne's breast shrieked at her as she spoke. Her fear - a black, screaming terror - gibbered at the thought of confronting the force behind the nightmare voice. This was a thing out of darkest dreams: something that could control dozens of minds.

Something that existed apart from humanity, yet seemed to dwell in it and warp people to its whims. How could she fight that: something that had no body?

Yet as those thoughts ran in a terrified little circle at the center of Anne's being, she found herself calming. It didn't matter - couldn't matter - what the outcome was here. It only mattered that this thing wouldn't claim Chelle. The mind behind the voice might not have a body, but there was at least a face in front of Anne now.

And she'd spent several years of her life pounding on people on her sister's behalf.

Anne whipped a feint at the man-shaped thing on the left. It drifted away, and a fistful of skeletal fingers from the center monster wrapped around her wrist. Anne snapped her free hand down, holding the thing in contact. The honeyed luminescence clothing her hands hardened, trapping the insectile digits in photonic amber. Anne lifted her feet from the cold stone floor and let her weight pendulum from its arm.

She drove her foot down and into the outside of its knee. A flash of auric glory etched lines deep on her opponent's face, and Anne felt drawn-wire tight ligaments stretch past their limits and tear. Pallid lips skinned back from its ebony snarl. A series of detonations as it ground its teeth to breaking announced to their tiny world that these abominations could feel pain.

Her feet met the floor, one on stone and one on a shattered mass of bone and tissue. As soon as she landed, Anne grounded her heel and drove her elbow toward the creature's exposed jaw. On contact, another flash of light accompanied the snap of breaking bone and the dull pop as the joint separated mixed nauseatingly and rolled back up through her shoulder. Before, her stomach had turned at dealing that kind of damage, but hurting these things just fanned the flames of her spirit.

Anne's world abruptly slowed, and she knew without seeing that a stiffened knife hand tipped with cruel, black claws drove toward her unguarded back. Simultaneously, the thing to her front was throwing the same blow at the ribs under her arm. If both strikes landed, Anne would be out two functioning lungs. More importantly, Chelle would be left at the tender mercies of whatever was behind this hideous display. It was fortunate then, that Anne had no intention of letting either creature gets its claws inside her tender skin.

It was far easier to move in the direction one already faced. Anne leaned to her right and slid her left foot back, driving her weight through her other foot and into the ruined knee of the center creature. As the monster to her front drifted around its falling companion, Anne arched her back to dodge its strike. Her hands curled around that slowly floating arm and snapped shut.

Anne cranked herself around, using the man-thing's arm as a lever. She drove her shoulder into its chest and threw it into the path of its fellow. She heard a meaty thud and felt pricking against her deltoid where it contacted the thing's chest. Anne sprang away and saw the thing she'd released slowly slump forward. It slid off the clawed hand of the one behind it with a sickening sucking noise.

The thing looked down at its fingers, covered in the fluids of its sibling. The shifting pearlescent light washed out whatever color the ichor might have, turning it black in Anne's sight.

"Tell me, wicked child, do you know how rare it is to find three of one kind?" Its unnatural eyes snapped up, its gaze lancing out to spear Anne's with a burning hatred made all the more virulent for the creature's motionlessness. "Three beautiful male children, all intelligent and sensitive. They came to me. They chose to serve, to gain greater beauty by my will." Anne's mind reeled at the thought of willingly subjecting oneself to such a malevolent psyche.

"And between you and that one, in mere moments, you have destroyed the work of centuries!"

"Perhaps you shouldn't have fed off those who hadn't asked for it," Anne panted. Out of the corner of her eye, she saw Chelle still dancing. It didn't appear she'd paused at all. Her sister's chest heaved, and a sheen of sweat showed on her exposed skin. Chelle's eyes were no longer shut, but stared wide open at nothing. The flickering light of Under Hill danced over them in a way that set Anne's heart aching.

The unman left standing shrieked, a piercing scream full of the rage of dying stars.

"You all ask for it! Every moment of every day do you yearn to be made better! With every lapsed plan, every failed calling, every dream sublimated to unlovely reality, you and all your kine beg me to take your grubby little souls in my fist!" The mind ruling the thing twisted its face into a parody of a person, the petty hatred molding the noble features with the inchoate frustration of a thwarted child. "You want someone else to make you dance, to make you sing. Every one of you desires to abrogate your agency to another, to someone better. I am better, and yet you resist!"

The desperate frustration set Anne aback. So many people she knew, practically everyone she met: every one of them asking why someone else didn't fix things. Why won't the president make it better? Or if not the president, the mayor, the governor or someone else in power. The implication was that if someone else takes care of the problems, then I don't have to, and can get on to more important issues.

For a moment, Anne's guard slipped.

And in that moment, the will moving the unman struck.

Smokey shadow wreathed the thing, and it blurred in Anne's vision. There was a flash of golden light in the midst of a suddenly Stygian darkness. Anne felt a thud, and somehow found herself flying through the air. She had a confused image of Chelle floating over the top of her, starshine limning her short, spiky hair and a rictus grin fixed on her unseeing face, and Anne felt the impact of her shoulders on the obsidian.

She slid across the ice-slick stone, coming to a rest hanging just over the ledge. For one endless instant, the moonstone shimmer of what passed for a ceiling spun over her head. Anne's lizard brain jabbed her in the metaphorical backside, and her spasming diaphragm contracted, dragging an implosion of air into her lungs.

A darkening shadow overhead sent Anne rolling back across the volcanic glass. A smoky figure dropped out of the gloom, an echoing crack resounding from the hard surface where Anne's head had just lay.

Anne rolled to her feet, and it was only instinct that had her sway to her right. The unman flew past her, clawed hands outstretched to rend and tear. The breeze from the last thing's passage ruffled her hair. Streaming shadowy vapor, it rolled and came to its feet.

"The hide from your flesh," the unman shrieked. "The flesh from your bones!"

The thing charged, its horrific visage drawing closer with unnaturally smooth grace. Wicked claws reached out of the inky mist it wore as a cloak, grasping for not just her flesh, but her soul as well.

Anne should have been terrified. Indeed, her fear sent galvanizing threads weaving through her chest, but they twined together with furious, incandescent anger, driving Anne forward to meet her hellish adversary.

Anne was glad she'd chosen to wear her flat-soled boots to this vile pit of a club: though she loved the inches heels gave her, she'd never have been able to fight in them, let alone run on the slick stone.

Chelle spun between them as the howling anathema bore down on her, and Anne's heart skipped a beat. Her sister leapt into the air, spinning to leave a bare hair's breadth as the the creature roared past, and Anne had time only to move.

At the last instant, Anne threw herself to her knees in front of the monstrous thing howling for her blood. The insensate rage on its perverted face betrayed a surprising lack of control. She must have irritated the will that drove it.

Anne leaned back nearly prone as she slid across the mirror-polished stone. She took a sketchy kick on one hip, but she could tell she'd surprised her enemy, as the wild blow had no force. She snaked out her trailing hand and caught the thing by one bony ankle. Anne used the thing's momentum against it, pulling hard on its leg, simultaneously spinning her around and whipping the unman face first into the obsidian with all the strength of its wild charge. Anne quashed any sympathy she felt at the hollow crack as skull bounced off stone.

Anne sprang to her feet, and Chelle leapt over the prone unman, inverted, unsupported, her body turning in the air. Her sister's shining form hung suspended over the collapsed monster, and a flash of insight nearly blinded Anne. Her sister still danced, the crowd still gyrated, the musicians still played at the same fever pitch.

Whatever the will was, it didn't control anything but her

opponents. It inspired, it drove them, but it was only as powerful as they allowed. Anne hadn't given it an opening. Her mind was too disciplined; her character too honed toward protection. Sudden confidence burned like an ember at Anne's core. Chelle might still dance, but she'd always danced. The thing that ruled Under Hill didn't own her. Not yet, at least.

Not ever.

Chelle passed over the downed creature and landed, spinning away in a blurring series of pirouettes that made Anne's head spin in sympathy, as the last unman rose from the obsidian, its smoky cloak distorting its form. And Anne stalked forward to meet it.

The light around Anne's hands flared again, hardening as she drove a fist into the center of the wavering mass. The occulting shadowy mirage fled before her blow, revealing pale skin over lean flesh. The strike thudded into the unman, accompanied by a puff of evaporating darkness.

The thing's face, nose grotesquely flattened by its impact with the stone altar, twisted into a grimace of mixed pain and effort. A claw whipped out of the wavering cloak, and Anne wasn't quick enough to dodge. The raking blow landed on her shoulder, rocking her to the side. It was accompanied by the now-familiar golden flash, and the unman howled in frustration and pain. Anne rolled with the blow, and slammed another radiant blow into the thing's side, dispersing more of its protective umbra.

For desperate moments, they traded strikes, dodging and weaving. Each time Anne hit the unman, a bit more of its cloaking darkness dissipated. Every blow she took rocked her with unnatural strength, but the flaring light kept its wicked claws out of her flesh. Around them, Chelle spun and leapt.

Despite the cool darkness of Under Hill, sweat plastered Anne's hair to her her head and made tracks down her spine and between her breasts. Her chest heaved, sucking air into tired lungs. The repeated blows should have been bone breaking, but her unseen protector robbed them of force. She could still feel the bruises, however, and they were starting to take a toll.

Finally, the Anne slipped sideways, snapping a short kick at unman's leg. It stumbled forward, and she pivoted, driving her knee into its lower back with all the strength of her powerful legs.

The unman fell to its knees and reared back, its spine arching as it shrieked in consuming agony. Anne drove her fist downward, striking at the point where the thing's collarbones met its sternum. The snap of bone echoed in the suddenly still air.

Anne rode the blow down, striking through the target as she'd been taught, but thrusting the unman all the way prone to the obsidian stone surface. She pinned it to the volcanic glass, and the fight - and its horrific facsimile of life - went out of it. Pallid lids fluttered down over those soulless metal eyes and the cruel lines and hard planes relaxed, giving Anne a brief glimpse of what the unman might have been before submitting itself to the will that had given it shape.

Anne stood and blinked her eyes as the battle fury drained from her. She could feel every blow the vile trio had landed. She wanted to sleep for a week.

"Annie?" Trepidatious disquiet suffused Chelle's voice. Confusion and no small amount of fear lurked in her sister's beautiful eyes. Deep circles smudged purple under those eyes, and her oval face was all hard planes, reminding Anne strongly of Ryan. Chelle stood at the edge of the obsidian floor looking small and worn.

Anne looked down at herself, stunned to see the golden luminescence crawling over her body. It seemed to describe planes and solids, making it look as though she wore a suit of transparent amber armor. It was beautiful, and more than a little disturbing.

Anne opened her mouth to reply when a piercing keen shook the club. It was as though Anne had a tornado siren planted between her ears. The howling shriek was a physical force, and she was vaguely aware of falling to her knees, and of Chelle and the everyone else in her field of vision doing the same. For a moment, Anne thought her vision was blurring, but then she realized that the blocks upon which she knelt were actually shaking.

"Chelley," she screamed, as the room started to come apart.

When Chelle didn't respond, Anne scrambled across the heaving blocks toward her. Anne slid to a stop and wrapped her arms around her sister, heaving them both to their feet. They slide-stepped around the jouncing form of the dead unman, desperately trying to stay on their feet.

As she pulled them toward the stairs up, Anne noticed that everyone else seemed to have the same idea. She could see the former prey of the parasitic sentience awakening. Many were screaming. Most scrambled their own slip-sliding way to the stairs. No few seemed completely catatonic.

A particularly violent heave of the floor sent Anne to her knees. Her hand flew open and the lucky coin bounced away, disappearing into the swirling crowd. A pang of loss shot through Anne's core, as well as a flash of incandescent fear. Anne suppressed them both with the ease of long practice, and lifted Chelle back to her feet. They dashed for the stairs, moving in an odd bubble of space with the crowd flowing to either side.

"You!" The word encompassed a world of frustration, pain and anger. Anne saw frightening club owner appear out of the crowd at the bottom of the stairs, blocking their way out. More imprecations tumbled from its lush lips in that nauseatingly mellifluous voice. "You unlovely harridan! You creator of nothing! You destroyer of beauty!"

Anne's will crystallized. With one arm, she picked up Chelle, not thinking that her sister easily massed three-quarters of her own weight. Anne charged toward the ranting figure, determination evident in each stride.

"You dare fight me? In my place? Under Hill is me, pathetic worm! You have no more hope of escape than of beating-"

Anne reached the blockading thing-in-human-form and drove her fist upward. Unexpectedly, that golden blaze coalesced around her arm again, just as she struck the club owner. Whose furious mouthing ceased as though cut off with an axe. The slight, androgynous figure of the club owner flew backward to crash upon the steps, and Anne swept Chelle up and over, taking the steps three at a time.

The mass of the crowd behind carried them up and through the antechamber, which had changed drastically since Anne went down the stairs. The room was devoid of decoration. Bare cinderblock walls enclosed the space, covered with slimy mold that oozed downward to puddle on the floor. A floor covered in the detritus of the city. Food wrappers, newsprint, unidentifiable plastic and leaves. Bits of rotting food, and dead rats. It was disgusting, and Anne swore it hadn't been there on the way in, though it looked to have been undisturbed for weeks, or even months.

The door was the only thing the same. That heavy, ironbound oak door. It hung open, the enormous ogre of a bouncer nowhere to be found. Anne dragged Chelle through the yawning portal, certain her friends had some explaining to do. Avi might not have known - probably didn't, to be honest - that Under Hill was some kind of twisted fairy hell place. But Mike had a notion. He knew something, and she knew he did.

What had happened down there? What were those things, and where had the club gone? And what was Mike's lucky coin? What the hell was happening in her city?

WIZARD TRAINING

VINCENT STARED AGAIN AT THE HANDS THAT HAD BETRAYED HIM. They'd once danced to his will and produced music to make proud men weep. No longer, though they looked no different than they had a few days earlier.

Nails kept short and well-filed. He'd used to chew them to the quick - until he bled - before he realized their ragged unevenness drove him to distraction. Basic hygiene training had done for that.

Blunt tips padded thickly with callus enabled him to handle the hottest of dishes with little ill-comfort. More importantly, he'd been able to play for hours. Long enough that muscle fatigue forced him to stop. He hadn't had a practice blister in years.

Long fingers sprang from broad palms. He'd been chastised often enough by his instructors over them. Not for merely possessing them. No, he'd been able to wrap his hands so far around the neck of his violin that he'd become lazy. Certain tough fingerings lost any difficulty.

Vincent's lips quirked at the old, familiar thought that perhaps some of his teachers had been more jealous than anything else. After all, he'd early graduated to pieces that he knew still challenged some of them.

His smile turned bittersweet. More bitter than sweet, truthfully: they'd never have to worry about him again. The fingers of his right hand, his bow hand, curled into a tight fist around the emblem of that horrible night.

"What's the matter, Vinnie?"

His mother's voice jerked Vincent out of the dark morass his thoughts had become in recent days. He stared at her in disbelief. Not over the nickname. She'd called him Vinnie since before he could remember. She wasn't going to stop anytime soon.

"Dr. Thomas said you haven't been to class in days."

Vincent scowled at his fingers. Dr. William Thomas was Vincent's violin tutor. A superlative musician who'd retired from touring in order to teach and record, Dr. Thomas had become almost a second father. The prospect of disappointing him plowed raw furrows in Vincent's bleeding soul.

"I can't play anymore, Ma." His voice cracked and black despair washed through him at the admission. He'd managed to not say anything about it since the agonizing episode nearly two weeks earlier, and saying it out loud left a screaming void in Vincent's middle.

"I know what you lost," his mother whispered, her voice harsh. Then she laughed, low in her throat. It was her voice - she was the only other person in the entire apartment - but she'd never used that tone that he'd ever heard. It wormed its way deep into his mind and left slimy trails of innuendo.

Vincent's head snapped up to stare in horror at his mother. A brief shadow passed over her familiar face, and she looked at him with the same calm expression she usually wore.

"What did you say?" His voice cracked on the last word, and he swallowed convulsively, trying desperately to work moisture into his bone-dry mouth.

"I said, Vinnie, Sweetie, are you feeling all right?" His mother's dark eyes were full of concern for him, as they often seemed of late, and she'd twisted her apron into a knot around her hands.

Vincent stared hard at her.

"Didn't you hear me, Ma?" Vincent almost shouted. "I. Can't. Play. Violin."

His mother's mouth worked in silence for a moment.

"What do you mean, Vinnie? Are you hurt, or sick? What's preventing you from playing?"

"I, I don't know." Vincent stared into nothing, thinking back to that nightmarish episode at the nightclub he should never have been at in the first place. Images flashed across his vision. Heartrendingly beautiful music in a place out of a dream, full of enormous trees. Dancers so graceful they made him weep to watch. They'd all played in time, shifting back and forth in tempo and dynamic without conscious thought. Melody, harmony, counter-melody wove through each other seamlessly. It had been transcendent.

And then a figure limned in golden light brought the illusion crashing down. Their music - his music - had been glorious, but it was the burning of a firework. A magnificent fireball that consumed its fuel and disappeared. And after the screaming exodus from the dank pit the club had transformed into, Vincent had found he couldn't play.

"Well, have you tried?" His mother used the sweet, patient tone she always used when she thought Vincent was being stubborn.

His jaw clenched and his fingers knotted into fists, but when he spoke, his voice was hushed.

"When I pick up the violin," not *his* violin, not anymore, "it feels strange. I can't finger chords. The bow doesn't work right, and the notes don't come out pure." He stared, unseeing, at the floor. The pattern in the worn, yellow linoleum was so familiar, he could have drawn it in his sleep, but just then it was dark and alien. Ominous. He swallowed past the enormous lump in his throat. "My hands don't even know how to hold a violin anymore."

Lines of worry appeared in his mother's face, but they only echoed the yawning abyss in Vincent's heart. She opened her mouth when the doorbell rang, making them both jump. The sounds was clangorous in the hushed apartment.

"Oh, that's Dr. Thomas." The relief in her voice was gratingly apparent.

Vincent knew his mother loved him, but she'd never been able to handle conflict, especially when she didn't understand the source. He didn't understand the source of his turmoil, for that matter, but he knew his raw emotions were making her uncomfortable. He just didn't care. Couldn't care.

Vincent inhaled, not smelling the rich aroma of pasta carbonara heavy on the air. Nor did he smell the fear-cold sweat that sprang onto his face, though his mouth tasted of ashes and pain.

"I thought he might be able to help you, so when he called, I asked him to come over for dinner." A hint of old fear showed in her dark eyes when Vincent sprang to his feet. "You know, honey, to talk to you."

"How- but-" Vincent's mind shuddered and caromed from thought to thought, galvanized by sudden terror. His thoughts shattered and flew apart at at the image of trying to explain to his mentor why he couldn't make music.

Deeper, much farther down in his soul, a molten hot pool of rage simmered and roiled. He shouldn't have to explain a damn thing. He shouldn't have to look forward to a life of asking fat-faced idiots if they wanted fries with their burger. He should be preparing for the winter concert season, and gearing up for his senior recitals.

"I'll- I'll just get the door," his mother offered in a suddenly quavering voice. The fear behind her words momentarily snapped Vincent back to the semblance of a normal frame of mind. With a shock, he realized he was looking down at her. His mother always seemed the giantess of his earliest hazy memories. Somehow, she'd turned into a rather short, slender woman in her late thirties when he wasn't paying attention.

The sound of the front door opening energized Vincent. He heard his mentor's deep voice raised in greeting, and knew he had to move. He just couldn't face Dr. Thomas. Not now. He knew he'd have to do it sometime, but now he just hurt too damn much.

Vincent grabbed his jacket and stuffed it in his army surplus, drab-green backpack and opened his bedroom window. As he ducked out onto the fire escape, he heard Dr. Thomas' voice, distant and muffled from the walls between then.

"Vincent. I know what you lost," the normally warm bass grated across Vincent's nerves, chilling the blood in his veins, "and I can give it back to you."

He scampered down the iron ladder as quickly as his rigid muscles would allow. Anything to get away from those words, spoken by familiar voices with an utterly alien tone.

Vincent felt better once he got onto the street and lost himself in the rhythms of the city. He rode the subway downtown and then just walked. Shoulders rubbed his, clad in everything from designer silk to stained, stinking canvas. His habits of movement took control, sliding him into gaps in the crowd as the uncounted urbanites surged and flowed in rush-hour foot traffic.

He didn't really know how long he wandered. This far north, sundown was hours off yet, even if the autumnal cool was enough for him to appreciate the jacket he'd snatched in his haste.

The phone in his pocket vibrated again, sending an unpleasant buzz up his arm nearly to the elbow. He'd nearly answered it the first time, just as he'd neared the shadowy entrance to the subway station nearest the apartment. He'd taken the time to compose an apology to his mother and Dr. Thomas for ditching out, and he'd be home after he'd done some thinking. They hadn't stopped calling.

That wasn't what set his hands to shaking in his pockets, though.

They'd sent text messages, too. Several each. Buried in them were bolded words that set Vincent's heart racing and turned his steps nearly into a stagger. I. Know. What. You. Lost. Vincent. He'd have dismissed them, but one was from a classmate who had no way to know.

He thought he'd just misheard his mother. He'd managed to convince himself that Dr. Thomas hadn't said the same thing. Until that horrifying message inside the messages. Now he thought he might be going crazy. Wasn't that one of those clinical symptoms: seeing patterns where none really existed?

Vincent heard the sound of a distant violin and his heart spasmed in his chest. The player was good, but not as good as he'd been. And never would be again. The sprightly music danced toward him from somewhere ahead. He knew he couldn't face the player, or even listen to the song anymore.

Vincent changed direction abruptly. A Sikh skipped backward, startling a woman in a long dress carrying a tiny puffball of an eye-searing pink. Which was apparently alive, as it set up a raucous yapping when she gasped. The street-goers swirled for a moment from the chaos of Vincent's motion, and a man in a rumpled suit cursed at him when Vincent stepped on his toes. Then he was into the street.

Playing dodge-em in rush hour traffic on the downtown streets didn't take much more than quick reflexes. He'd gotten lucky in his timing, and the closest light was still red as he slipped between the stationary vehicles. The biggest danger was the city's normal mob of taxis, but even they did no more than honk as he ran past.

Vincent skipped up onto the sidewalk on the far side, and lost himself in the press of humanity for long enough to get out of even the possibility of earshot of the unseen violinist. Several blocks later, when he slipped to the edge of the sidewalk near a streetlamp to pause for breath, he realized he'd somehow gotten all the way to Carnegie Hall.

Which was strange, as he'd have sworn he wasn't anywhere near it when he got off the subway at 23rd Street. He looked around, hunching his shoulders. He felt odd. Not just the unending agony in his soul that came from a shattered identity. He felt physically strange.

"I know what you've lost, Vincent."

The rough voice behind him made Vincent leap nearly out of his skin. He turned slightly to see a cab driver staring out of his taxi. Vincent's blood ran cold as the words registered. The cabbie stared at him with dead, black eyes that reminded Vincent of a shark he'd seen at the aquarium.

Vincent stood rooted to the spot, staring back at the driver - an otherwise unprepossessing man in worn clothing - mind blank with horror. A distant part of him saw the passenger in the back of the cab pounding on the plexiglass divider with one hand, while the vehicles behind the taxi set up a furious clamor.

"Why'd you run from your mother, Vincent?" The cabbie's face, lined from age and care stretched into an unnaturally wide grin that set Vincent's stomach to roiling. "And Dr. Thomas, who only wants to help you, Vincent. Why?"

A wave of despair and terror shrank Vincent's skin on his bones. He ached to run from the horrible thing in front of him, but he couldn't move. His muscled had seemingly turned to wax and wouldn't respond.

"I want to help you, too, Vincent."

The cabbie's face twitched, the horrid rictus-smile sliding off his pouchy features. His eyes blinked rapidly, and in a moment between blinks, changed from soulless pits into the eyes of a irritable, old man. One who took in Vincent, his angry fare and the even angrier drivers behind him and made an easy choice of targets.

"What're you staring at, punk?" The man's Brooklyn accent - along with the proffered middle digit - went ill at odds with the rest of the short exchange, doing nothing to ease Vincent's fear and growing paranoia. The cabbie finally responded to the press of traffic and sped off, and only then did Vincent's muscles unknot. He staggered back into crowd moving down the sidewalk, drawing irritated looks from those forced to accommodate his almost spastic progress.

Vincent's worn nerves were frayed nearly to breaking. First with his sudden inability to play, and now something seemed to be following him. Except it wasn't - couldn't be - human. It controlled people. Controlled his own mother! It made them say what it wanted them to, do what it wanted them to.

And it wanted him, for some reason.

Or, it was just a figment of his imagination, and he was somehow going certifiably insane. Somehow, the thought made him chuckle. Better that, than a horrible monstrous presence chasing him.

"That's-"

"Not-"

"A nice-"

"Thing-"

"To say-"

"Vincent."

Six different heads of six different passersby rotated to address him. Each in turn, though their feet never stopped. Each with shark-dead black pits of eyes. Six different heads shifted back, giving no indication that their owners had any idea what had just happened.

The bottom dropped out of Vincent's stomach, while his head felt as though it was a mile up in the air. The fact that he hadn't eaten anything all day impressed itself dimly on his tenuous awareness, and a surge of atavistic terror drowned the brief moment of dark humor.

Vincent ran.

Shouted curses followed as he bumped and collided with individual members of the crowd. Vincent didn't have enough self-consciousness left to apologize. His pulse surged. Breath rasped in his throat. Faces and storefronts blurred into a homogenous mess of color and matter. It didn't matter. None of it mattered, so long as he got away.

And over it all, he heard that damned voice.

"Vincent," it called in dozens of voices, but always with that same rough, rasping, mocking tone. "I know what you lost, Vincent," it sang. "I know what was taken from you."

Sweat, at once both hot from exertion and cold from his fear, ran into Vincent's eyes. He didn't notice the sting of the salt, didn't notice the burn in his legs from the unaccustomed exercise. Tight fisted hands flailed on the ends of his arms as he fled. His feet flapped against the hard sidewalk as he tried desperately to escape. If only he could fly.

An ungentle quiet hushed the normal sounds of the city. Vincent still heard car horns blaring, still heard the mutter of humanity, but only distantly. Even the wild thudding of his pulse and the coughing panting of his breath were no more than a sullen background thrum, mixed and woven through the heartbeat of crowded civilization.

"Vincent!"

Soulless ebon pits and a wolfish grin out of place in the familiar mahogany face of Dr. Thomas leapt into stark focus out of the exertion-blurred background of the street. A wave of bone-deep cold swept over Vincent, and his vision darkened. The air turned oven-hot, parching his open mouth. Vincent smelled the lifeless dust, and his heart shuddered. His mentor's features took on a bestial cast, his nose snout-like and his ears long and oddly squared off.

Vincent cried out, and threw up a hand as the ghastly form of his friend reached for him with claw-like fingers. The crowd around him turned slowly, so slowly, as though they moved through molasses. The thrumming of the city crescendoed, beating on his ears in oppressive waves of inchoate noise.

Vincent's foot slipped.

The shroud that had fallen over his world unaccountably brightened, taking on a gilt appearance. It felt to Vincent as though the pavement itself had moved out from under his sneaker. His sense of balance shifted, tilted, and was gone. He reeled sideways away from the monster Dr. Thomas had become, working just to keep his feet under him.

Vincent caromed off the pedestrians around him as he staggered. He felt each jarring impact as he thudded from person to person. He had just enough awareness of his surroundings to feel a delicate layer of purely mundane apprehension over the numbing terror as he noticed himself clip a policeman on his careening path around the corner of the block.

"Vincent!"

Dr. Thomas' voice was still the abrasive roar of whatever it was that chased him, but Vincent detected a note in it he hadn't heard before. Anger. The abomination of man and beast his mentor had become was angry, and Vincent realized he was somehow leaving it behind.

The world around Vincent snapped back into focus, the darkening shroud dropping away. The sounds of the metropolis rushed into blasting volume from the overbearing stillness that held reality momentarily at bay. Sour sumac and auto exhaust crowded into his nostrils, and the sheer, vibrant life of the city was enough to pull a cry of relief out of Vincent's abused throat.

Both his cry and the background noise cut off again as he fell headlong through an open doorway. One which snapped shut as he fell in a heap on the scarred, wooden floor. For a long, quiet moment, Vincent simply lay on the floor and shook. When cruel claws and savage teeth didn't close on his flesh, his heart began to slow from the brutal pace to which fear and action had driven it. Vincent sobbed quietly from reaction, his abused mind barely active.

"Not many are that desperate to get into my shop, youngster."

Vincent rolled to a sitting position, still panting, and looked up at what he presumed was the shopkeeper. And stared. The man who leaned on the polished countertop smiling down at him must have been nearly seven feet tall. He looked like a cartoon caricature. A feathering of raven-black hair that stuck out nearly around his shiny, bald crown. His lined skin was the yellow of aged ivory Vincent saw in the antiquities section of the museum, and looked to have the texture of fine vellum.

Vincent focused on his face and almost gasped. Air whistled into his nostrils as the muscles along his jaw bunched. The man's gazed at him with black eyes. A bare second later, Vincent castigated himself. The skeletal shopkeeper possessed heavy eyelids, and his smile gave the impression that he had little in the way of whites to those watching eyes.

Besides, this man's eyes were full of life, bright with personality and interest. Not dead and soulless like whatever had been chasing him. They sat close to a nose that should have dwarfed every other feature the man owned, as it swept out and down from his eyebrows in a smooth curve. It fit, though Vincent wasn't certain how.

"Ah, I-" Vincent began, and realized he had no idea how to make what he'd experienced sound at all possible, let alone plausible. Not to mention sane.

"Mmmmm. There is licorice and mint tea in the carafe," he gestured with one long-fingered hand to a brushed steel pitcher on a small table that appeared to be made from a section of a fluted marble pillar, then cocked his head to one side and blinked. "Why don't you look around, young sir. Those who find their way here usually have a need to." With that odd pronouncement, he left the counter and disappeared back into the bookshelves that swallowed the little shop.

Vincent stared after him, as yet unable to make sense of the encounter. He sat on the floor, legs folded under him and leaning on one fist, for what felt like ages. With one still-trembling hand, he pulled his phone out of his pocket. He had the vague idea of letting his mother know where he was, but two things stopped him. He had no idea where he actually was, and more importantly, he didn't have service.

He slipped the phone back into his pocket, then rubbed the sweat off his face. Cool air flowed gently over his exposed skin, carrying with it a bewildering array of scents. There was the peculiar scent of old paper, but also leather and oil. Some kind of flowery perfume teased his nose, along with the odd, incongruous smell of rich loam.

Vincent heaved himself to his feet. His exhausted muscles complained of their unaccustomed exertion, and he thought once again about how he should spend more time in a gym. Or outside. Or even just do some push-ups at home. Sourly, he thought he might even have the time now that he wouldn't be spending so much of his hours making music.

At a loss, Vincent cast about him. He stood in a space just large enough to stretch out in, bound on one side by the polished, wooden counter. Opposite that stood a glass case with a dozen books in various states of disrepair. Not a one was printed in English, and as Vincent looked closer, it looked like none of them had actually been printed at all.

The door to the outside world stood out. For one, it was just wood and glass. No bars and no visible lock, though Vincent had been moving too quickly on the way in to see whether there was a rolling gate. A large pane of frosted glass dominated, preventing him from seeing the people passing back and forth in front of it. For that matter, he couldn't see anything of city.

Set into the frosted window - backwards, from Vincent's perspective - were letters made of translucent stained glass in a myriad of brilliant colors. The letters cast light on the floor, and spelled out Mr. Judy's Rare Books.

Vincent swallowed and realized his throat was still parched from his run. He shuffled uncertainly over to the counter and picked up one of the paper cups in a stack next to the tea carafe. When he reached for the carafe with his other hand, he saw that it still clenched into a tight fist. He turned it over and frowned down at it. The tendons stood out, and he had to consciously force his fingers open. One more horrible thing in a horrible day, when his body started to refuse to cooperate.

His fingers open, he saw again the little gold coin he'd found in his pocket the day after his life ended. He had a flash of memory from that night, seeing the thing lying in the grass. It had glowed with bright light in the dim, nightmare place, and his hand had practically fallen on top of it when the floor shook. He must have picked it up then.

Vincent glared at it, all the fury he hadn't let out making a horrible din in his head. He'd come to hate the small disc as a symbol of whatever it was that had stolen his music. If anger had power, his fulminating gaze would have turned the worn, smiling face into slag. Light flashed off the surface of the little thing and right into his eyes. Vincent winced and stuffed the hated thing back in his pocket.

He poured a cup of the tea Mr. Judy had offered - it hadn't sounded like an offer, exactly - and sipped. The bookkeeper said licorice, but the tea tasted like no licorice he'd ever eaten. Herbal notes flowed together, and there was a lingering sweetness across his tongue that pair well with the mint.

The ache in his hand suggest he must have been clutching that damned coin since he'd left the house. He sipped again at the tea, letting the just-warm liquid sooth his raw throat.

A peculiar lassitude draped itself over Vincent's consciousness. It dawned on him that he hadn't had another visitation from whatever it was stalking him. Not since he'd fallen into the little shop. It was significant somehow, but he filed the thought away. It just didn't feel that immediate. Except for that moment of incandescent rage, even his anger and pain felt distant. Still there, just set apart for a bit.

He found himself wandering the narrow, book-choked aisles of the store. Shelves stood no more than a couple of feet apart, and went all the way to the ceiling. On those shelves seemed to be all the books of the world. Vincent noted titles as he passed. Many were books he'd read, or at least seen in stores and online. Most, however, were definitely not. Many titles he simply couldn't read, though he recognized Cyrillic lettering here, Chinese characters there, and something he thought might be Hindi.

Some he was certain were jokes. One was nothing but little triangles, some pointing up, some down and some pointing all over the place. Another seemed composed entirely of dimly seen shapes layered in clear plastic pages. Shapes that were deeper, somehow than the thin pages. Shapes that shifted depending on how he held the book in the odd, sourceless light of the very peculiar bookshop.

Vincent wasn't aware how long he wandered the shelves, but there always seemed to be another aisle with more books. After the hell his life had become, the sense of great age and wisdom from that much collected knowledge eased his heart in a way he couldn't have predicted. Constant mental agony had worn grooves in his thinking, but the influence of the quiet shop was pulled him out.

He began to wonder, vaguely, what he would do now that the future he'd expected was closed to him. He had to find some way to make a living. Music was about all he knew. Maybe he could conduct. The thought of being that close to violinists pricked at the languor suffusing his awareness. The military always needed healthy bodies.

Vincent's feet dragged him to a stop and a portion of the drowsy veil lifted. He stood just down from a door he'd passed a few times, but hadn't actually noticed. A thick stone plaque in the middle of the heavy wooden door told him not to enter. A thought not entirely his own insinuated that this was for his own good. And the world's.

Unconsciously, he shivered and turned to look at the shelf to his left.

In marked difference from the rest of the shelves, the books on this one had been arranged to create a small cubby, no more than a foot on a side. Inside that space, on a plush platform lay a single book. The leather than bound it might once have been a creamy white, but age and use had turned the cover a deep, golden yellow. He saw no title on, on either the front or the spine, but each corner bore a heavy-looking metal decoration, with bits cut out. Any more delicate, and they'd look like lace, but they were ... too substantial, almost like they weighed more than they should.

Vincent slipped the empty cup into his jacket pocket, and picked the book up without a thought. It felt curiously light in his hand for such a large book. It more than filled his hand. Curiously, the cover formed a box, completely enclosing the pages. He ran a finger down the edge and tugged. With a barely perceivable click, the cover released. He opened it and as his eye hit the first page, time stopped. He was conscious of drawing a deep breath, the taste of the tea still light on his tongue, the smell of old books, flowers and fresh earth heavy in his nostrils.

Then, it seemed as though he awoke from a deep sleep. He caught himself as his knees started to buckle. He snapped the book shut in reflex and stood trembling. His heart thudded as rapidly as it had when he'd first entered the store. It came to Vincent in a rush that he had no idea how long he'd been in Mr. Judy's shop; no idea where the bookstore even was. Moreover, as long as he was there and without phone signal, his mother had no way to contact him. And vice versa.

"I need to get home."

The voice, his own, startled him in the hushed place, and Vincent abruptly turned and walked toward where he thought the front counter should be. Should be, as he really wasn't certain he was right. It felt like everything that had happened since he'd first fallen through the door had happened in a dream, or to someone else.

Fortunately, it didn't seem to matter, as the second turn left him standing in front of Mr. Judy's counter. Behind which stood Mr. Judy, who somehow managed not to loom over Vincent's slightly bewildered form.

"You've found something then! I am surprised. Most people don't see that volume at all, let alone get so absorbed." The attenuated proprietor's rich voice filled the space around them without rising above a whisper, but the enthusiasm in his words brightened his black eyes.

Eyes that picked out the absurdly light book still in Vincent's hand. Who started, nearly dropping the precious item in the process, and stared in mixed surprise and shock at his hand. When he transferred his stunned gaze to the shopkeeper, black eyebrows just as feathery as his hair climbed high onto the shiny dome in interest.

"Or, I dare say, it's found you, hmmm?" Mr. Judy turned his head so that he was looking at Vincent through a single eye. His aquiline nose jutted out of his face, giving the old man's face an oddly inhuman cast. "Or is it perhaps that you don't want the Primer after all?"

"I, I-" Vincent knew he shouldn't buy it, especially when he and his mother wouldn't be able to afford to send him to school if his scholarship got pulled. But he found himself determinedly unwilling to put the book back where he'd found it. Or, as Mr. Judy said, it had found him. He swallowed and took a deep breath. "I want to take it with me. Please."

The lean bookseller planted his elbows on the counter and lowered his chin to rest on his folded hands. This put his head level with Vincent's, and he looked full into the younger man's eyes for a long, uncomfortable moment. Whatever he found there must have satisfied him, for at last a warm smile spread slowly across his angular face. He nodded.

"Yes, I think you shall have the book. It has been a long, long time since that was out in the world, but it seems you have need of it, and who am I to deny that need?"

He was silent for a long moment. Long enough for Vincent to begin to fidget. When he couldn't stand it anymore, Vincent spoke.

"How much do I owe you, Mr. Judy?" With a desperation that surprised him, Vincent hoped he could afford the price. Of its own accord, his free hand crawled into his pocket and found the unwanted gold coin. He wanted to get rid of the thing. He pulled it out and, barely glancing at the worn visage, offered it up. "Will this do?"

Mr. Judy surprised him with a booming laugh that by all rights should have set the books dancing on their shelves. For all that, it was gentle and in genuine good humor, and Vincent felt his spirits rise. He was surprised to find himself joining in. He hadn't had much laughter recently, and it felt good.

"Ah, no. Thank you," Mr. Judy said, graciously. "That is not for me, though I greatly appreciate the offer. As to the tome, pass it on when you know to whom you should. Otherwise, bring it back here, should you have the need. Until we meet again, fare you well, young magos."

Vincent had already turned away when he heard the odd form of address. He turned back to ask the proprietor what he meant by it, but the man had disappeared. Vincent blinked, and it came to him that the blessing had also been a form of dismissal.

He looked around the strange, little shop once more, then took the time to slip the gold coin back into his pocket. He opened the door and walked out into the early evening sun.

Which immediately dimmed, as the smell of long-dead and dusty air beat upon him. The sky above became a perfect eggshell-blue bowl, the sun a far-distant hammer. Tears streamed from Vincent's instantly dry eyes.

"There you are, Vincent." Dr. Thomas stood at the end of the street, while people crossed the intersection behind him. Cars and trucks drove, unconcerned by the unfolding drama. "It was unkind of you to run from your mother and me."

The older man took a step forward, and then another. Odd clicks accompanied each footfall, putting Vincent in mind of the time he'd accompanied his mother to a bank and a seeing-eye dog led its master across the polished, marble floor.

"Truly, Vincent, I only wish to help you regain what I know you've lost."

His heart twisted in his chest at the reminder of his music. All the thoughts held at bay inside Mr. Judy's came flooding back, and Vincent gasped at the raw strength of his emotions. The wan sunlight flashed off his mentor's glasses, and the older musician smiled, his normally blocky face appearing long and stretched through Vincent's tears.

"I can replace what that cold, northern monster took from you."

Vincent stood rooted to the pavement as Dr. Thomas stalked slowly forward. He gestured with the graceful hands that had always impressed Vincent, reaching toward the younger man as though in supplication. But now, Vincent could see the unnatural length of them, the long and jagged claws that tipped each digit.

Warmth in Vincent's hands, hotter even than the punishing rays of the alien sun overhead tore a hiss form his lips. He was surprised to feel the hard disc of the little coin in his right, having no memory of putting his hand back in his pocket, but he was purely shocked by the hot energy flowing up his arm from the book in his left hand.

"Vincent, put down the tome," the not-doctor growled. On more than one level. Vincent heard the familiar, trusted voice of his mentor, and under it, speaking the same words in unison, a bestial voice filled with rage. And hunger. A voice that continued, "don't you trust me, my boy?"

Two weeks sunk in despair had hollowed Vincent. He'd been unable to eat, to sleep. He'd barely functioned, flayed by his psychic agony and depression. He'd begun to question his sanity, and he'd even thought about killing himself. But now, this thing wanted him for its own purposes, and had spent the best part of a day terrorizing him. He was done.

Something in Vincent unfolded.

Half-seen images swirled in the kiln-like air around him. Lines and layers, like sheer fabric or flows of air in thick fog coated - everything. Thick, ropy strands of dark, shadowy something entangled the thing wearing his mentor's face - and God help it if it had hurt Dr. Thomas - writhing slowly like some horrific, bestial octopus. In the same way, Vincent sensed gleaming, gilded lines extending out from his hands. Angles and curves swooped away into a fading distance, growing dimmer as they went. It seemed much the way he'd always thought music should look.

"No." Alongside his newfound sight, Vincent's anger roared hot and clean. "I don't trust you."

The beast-thing stopped in its tracks, and Vincent could now see the re-curved legs. It looked less and less human as Vincent beheld more. The clicking he'd heard came from ragged claws on the ends of its paw-like feet, each the size of a dinner plate. Noisome breath whistled through yellowed teeth in an oddly bent snout. Deep-sunk eyes glowed with malevolent cunning under heavy, downward-sloping brows.

Cunning, but not with any great intelligence.

"But," the monster's voice combined all the worst tonal qualities of a contra-bassoon, a camel's bray and a cement-mixer full of broken glass and tone-deaf opera singers. He could barely hear its imitation of Dr. Thomas. A long, prehensile tongue the color of bread mold slithered between the thing's taut lips as it spoke. "I will help you become what you were." Thick, black drool dripped from its open maw, giving its offer the lie.

Whatever had opened inside Vincent continued, and he saw the creature in front of him for what it was. Massive, and monstrous, a hideous combination of man and mangy, feral beast. Ashen skin covered in patches of greasy, black hair was flecked here and there with furious, red boils and sores that wept an oily, green fluid. The creature was naked, except for tarnished metal rings around its upper arms and legs. Limbs thick with muscle nevertheless twitched and shook with noticeable palsy. It was demonstrably male, but bore a jagged, shiny patch of scar tissue between its legs.

"Come, my young pupil, let me give you the benefit of my experience," competed with, "so hungry, feast on your ka, magos," in Vincent's highly trained ears. He heard two overlaid sets of words every time the abomination spoke. It was the aural equivalent of the time he'd take a knock to the head and had double vision. And was just as disorienting.

Vincent's arms tingled with a heat that had nothing to do with the strange, desert sun the beast-creature brought with it. He'd never felt so full of life. His heart pounded as his thoughts buzzed with the power, and he began to look for a way to bend it to his will.

Without a conscious thought, Vincent's hand rose up, bearing the odd book from the odder book store. The cream leather cover blazed with a network of glowing vine-like knots, weaving and interweaving across its entire surface. Beams of light actually shown out of the crack in the boxlike covering, and it snapped open in his hand. Pages ruffled and blurred as they turned themselves.

Vincent's eyes rolled back in his head as images that he'd swear he'd seen before poured into the front of his mind in an incandescent way even music theory never had. Formulae, diagrams, lines and line of writing in a language he'd never seen, yet understood anyway, all jumbled together in his head. For one brief, infinite moment, Vincent saw the way everything fit together, and in that instant, his eyes snapped open.

He glared at the once-god before him.

The emasculated beast-thing's draw gaped and it roared at him. Legs - even stripped of most of its power as it was - coiled under it's not-insubstantial bulk flexed, and it shot into the air. Arms and jaws gaped wide, and though Vincent knew it was barely a shade of its former glory, he knew the monster could still consume him.

Those hideous, glowing eyes blazed with sulfurous triumph and black abyss followed in their wake, when Vincent's entire body tensed and he screamed. The energy blazing in his chest complied with his desire in a way he knew he'd likely never manage again. But now was enough.

The flows of energy and matter he sensed rearranged themselves to Vincent's will, coiling around into a channel that linked him to the erstwhile Typhonian. With a thought, Vincent sent the blazing, pure green energy of life he'd borrowed from the cosmos roaring down that empty channel in the flows of reality.

For an endless, fiery instant, Vincent looked into the heart of a god, saw the fall of an empire and the dwindling of self that accompanied it, and knew something of what was happening and why he'd suffered the devouring consumption of something for which he'd worked so hard.

And then time caught, restarted, and the very energy he'd summoned shouldered him aside, taking something of him with it. The hounding, desperate monster shrieked, locked in a blaze of energy inimical to its dark and chaotic existence. And then it frayed at the edges and began to crumble.

Vincent tried to cry out in triumph, but choking, oppressive silence suddenly reigned over the narrow street. With shocking suddenness that stopped his heart, the lines that made up existence warped and bubbled. Purple-black tentacles burst into being, converging on the struggling, disintegrating beast-thing, gripping it with horrific intimacy. They pulled the straining form into somewhere else, leaving Vincent alone on the horribly empty sidewalk.

Vincent's breath exploded out of him, and he gasped fresh air, unaware he'd been holding his breath at all. He retched with reaction, and staggered backward to lean against the brick wall behind him. The whole episode had his thoughts screaming around in tiny circles inside his skull.

Vincent's knees buckled and he slid to the sidewalk, suddenly aware of his crushing exhaustion. He remembered the whole day with crystal clarity, barring the strange fog he'd enjoyed inside Mr. Judy's not-really-there-maybe shop. He just couldn't quite recall how he'd done what he'd done after that.

Lifting the book of magic to his lap felt like hefting a couple of hundred pounds of lead brick. His eyes fluttered he was so tired. And hungry. He wanted to devour a couple of pizzas. Maybe three or four. His stomach growled in agreement.

"Hey, kid, you okay?"

Vincent's head rolled around to see his questioner. A short man in wearing a windbreaker over jeans and an athletic mesh shirt looked down at him. Shaggy, brown hair and brown eyes looked out of a tan face. Vincent's pulse sped up as the man reached into a pocket, but he heaved a sigh of relief as the man pulled out his wallet. When Vincent saw the polished brass of the badge attached to the inside, he thought distantly that his relief might be a little premature.

"I'm Detective Timmons, NYPD," the cop said in his tenor voice. "For now, at least," he muttered in with a bitter half-smile. He shook his head, dismissing whatever dark thought twisted his features. "Anyway, are you Vincent Bahur? 'Cuz Dr. William Thomas has been looking for a student of his."

Vincent opened his mouth to speak, but nothing came out. Fatigue crushed him where he sat, and ravenous hunger gnawed at his middle, but he tried again.

"Dr. Thomas is looking for me? I sent him a message."

Timmons looked down at him, one eyebrow raised.

"Kid, what Will said was you'd disappeared, and if I could put the word out, he'd appreciate it." The detective raised one hand in a placating gesture, using the other one to slip his wallet back into a pocket. "Now, I'm not calling you a liar, I'm just saying you might want to talk to the man face-to-face."

Vincent thought about what he'd seen, and the book still clutched in his hand, and how he'd treated his mother and his mentor.

"Yeah," he agreed. His stomach growled again. "I think I'd better. Can you give me a hand up, please? I think I need something to eat before I go home."

WITHIN RANGE

THE KID - VINCENT - WAVED AS HE WALKED UP THE STEPS TO THE first floor of the apartment building he and his mom lived it. Pat Timmons, sometime detective in the glorious NYPD waved back. As the kid disappeared into the building, Timmons' stomach turned over. The boy practically glowed with the power he'd drawn in. Spending time that close to him - and that book, whatever it was - felt like straddling a live power line.

No doubt Vincent thought Pat had just happened on him. Which was almost true. Dr. William Thomas, the boy's violin tutor, had called him when he and Vincent's mother found the note he'd left in his room, and given him a likely starting place. Which had helped, but once he'd gotten within a quarter mile or so, he'd been drawn to the kid like a magnet. The magic juice - whatever it really was, he had no clue - running through Vincent thrummed in the air. Pat couldn't help but feel it.

He'd always had a good bit of a sense of the genuine weirdness of the world. His granddad on his mom's side claimed it came from the Irish background. When Grandpa Murray talked about the Sight, you heard the capital letter. When something strange happened, Pat was sure to be around. It wasn't that he caused things, but they sure seemed to happen around him.

Especially since-

He shuddered, his breath suddenly coming fast and harsh. He hated the memories, feared them like nothing else in his life, but he rode them. It was the only way he knew to get through it. He was the master of his own damn soul.

†††

"Please! You have to help me! Those things got Carla!"

Pat had just stepped out of Convenient Willard's, where he'd stopped for some bait. Willard's was a little nook a few blocks from Chelsea Park, where Pat liked to go fishing for striped bass.

Right near midnight was about the only time he had available with his shift schedule. Fortunately, that meant the park wasn't terribly crowded. When he caught a good one, he treated himself to a dinner at the brewing company near Pier 59. Which wouldn't happen tonight, it seemed.

Pat estimated the young man was near twenty, of Middle Eastern descent and wearing jeans and a NYU sweatshirt. In deference to the cool of the night, he had a brown scarf wrapped around his neck. And naked panic splashed all over his face, made stark by the glare of the neon.

"Whoa, slow down, my friend. Who are you, who's Carla, what things," Pat asked. Then his eyes narrowed and he continued, "and what makes you think I'm a cop?"

"Uh, uh," the kid stammered, black eyes wide and glazed. "I'm Aram Kazemi. Carla's my, my girlfriend, and, and. They were - I don't know what they were! But they just, just appeared. Outta nowhere! And grabbed Carla and ran off to this boat!" Sweat sheened his face, though that could easily be from a run if he'd really come from the waterfront. He didn't read as a druggie, though Pat supposed his clothes could be hiding any needle tracks.

"Which way should we be going, here?" When Aram waved toward the nearby charter boat marina, Pat started moving. "And about me being a cop?"

"I, I fish at the park sometimes, and I've seen you there. I asked some of the other guys, and they told me."

Pat nodded. That might be possible. Aside from training, and Krav Maga practice, Pat had just enough time to do one thing to relax, and fishing was it. He spent that time at Chelsea. Usually around now, but often in actual sunlight on his days off. Some of the regulars knew

92

he was NYPD, but didn't bug him about it. It could come out in conversation, though.

"All right," Pat allowed, "what's this about things taking your girlfriend? What things?"

"They - oh, Jesus - they," the kid cut off. He stopped and bent over, planting his hands on his knees. His knuckles whitened as he gripped. "They looked like something out of a movie. Like, halfway between men and fish. And insects and lizards and God-knows-what! Covered in slime, with no noses, and black, staring eyes!"

With his description of the alleged kidnappers, Pat thought if the kid wasn't high on something, he'd do well in the theater department, assuming he actually was a student. Or writing some crazy sci-fi, if he wasn't.

"What were you two doing down at the waterfront this late at night?"

"I, uh," Aram flushed, "I'm a biology student-" answering that question "-and my term project involves tracking the striped bass population, and it lets me get some fishing time in, y'know?"

Pat did know, and said so, but that it still didn't explain what Aram and Carla were doing down at the docks near midnight. The restaurants were still open, but none of the marinas would be.

"Well, I spend a bunch of time down there, and I talk to the other guys who fish," Aram repeated. As the young man's terror ebbed, his flush deepened, "and, uh, a couple of them told me about this spot where you can, uh, not get disturbed. And, well, the acoustics keep people from hearing anything. And it's still kind of in public. The, uh, problem is you kind of have to sneak through part of the marina."

Pat's eyebrows shot up. Aram had the grace to look embarrassed.

"That's kind of trespassing, isn't it?" Pat made his voice coolly officious, though he genuinely didn't care one way or the other, so long as the kids didn't get caught or damage anything. Aram's words were as good as a confession, though, and Pat really didn't want to do the paperwork. Especially if this turned out to be some kind of student prank.

"Uhhh," Aram temporized.

"That's *if* the two of you had actually been in the marina after closing, right?" The trick was to stay cool and keep things hypothetical. If this *was* a kidnapping, though, everything would get very serious, very quickly.

"Uh, yeah." Aram blinked, dealing with the mental whiplash. He'd gotten his breathing under control, but his forehead still shone with sweat. "We, uh, we were *going* to, but we were still outside."

Which was good, as far as Pat was concerned, as intent wasn't legally actionable. Hell, he'd wanted to kill any number of people in his life, but hadn't done it.

"So, you and Carla were outside the marina," Pat said.

"Yes," Aram nodded, eyes glazing slightly. "We'd, ahh, just arrived," he paused, looking at Pat, "outside the marina, when I heard a noise." Aram's gaze went distant as memory caught him. "Carla sat up, and then some men burst it. At least I thought they were men." The blood drained from Aram's face, leaving a sickly pale greenish. His hands started shaking. "What do you get when you cross a frog, a fish and a man?"

Pat blinked, momentarily silenced.

"I don't know, Mr. Kazemi, what do you get?"

"I don't know, either, but four of them took my girlfriend." Aram turned and flashed a ghastly rictus grin. The look in his eyes nearly made Pat miss a step. The kid walked a knife-edge of horrified panic. And there was something else deep in his eyes that Pat couldn't identify.

The two men arrived at the pier. Pat stepped into the shadows to get out of the sparse foot traffic and beckoned Aram to join him. With his other hand, he reached into a pocket and pulled out his phone. Time to get in touch with his partner. Jaime Alcocer had been a cop nearly a decade longer than Pat. What the Puerto Rican detective from the barrio didn't know about police work would just about fill the back of postcard.

"Where about were you when Carla got snatched?" Pat looked out over the darkened marina, trying to pierce the gloom. And avoid the charming mélange of salt water and rotting garbage.

Aram giggled.

"Hey," said Pat, his voice sharp and low. "Keep it together while

I call this in and get some backup."

Pat heard the kid strangle a gasp and jerked his head up. The something dark in Aram's eyes grew stronger. Pat could see it even in the dark. Despair mixed with something else, something that looked almost like-

A sudden greasy stench assaulted his nostrils, a combination of dead fish, rancid oil and something alien. He coughed as that acrid alien reek caught at the back of his throat. A sense of presence behind him pulled his head around, and felt his eyes widen. A pit formed in his stomach, pulling a decade and a half of police experience down with it. Pat froze.

Aram hadn't lied.

A figure loomed out of the shadows, bulking large against the side of the building. At first, it - there was nothing about it to suggest it even had a sex - looked as though it wore some kind of armor, but it dawned on Pat that the thing's skin was made of plates of purplish chitin. It was nearly as wide as it was tall, and appeared squat against the mass of the warehouse, but Pat had to look up to see its face, which hung down over the front of the thing's chest.

Its face. A shudder of horror passed through Pat. Aram had been right, there, too. An obscene mix of frog, fish and man, the abomination's face showed pale, bluish skin with a spattering darker spots the same color as its carapace, all covered in some kind of shiny slime. Pallid gills in its neck flared in a regular pulse, and even paler lips stretched wide across a narrow jaw.

It was as though someone had taken a man's face, wiped off the features leaving only the eyes, and opened a mouth just under the jawline. A mouth that gaped open, filled with inward-pointing, conical teeth. Like the eel the thing resembled, Pat saw an inner set of jaws as it opened its maw to hiss at him.

The smell of its breath went beyond stench to a place of sublime horror. Pat's stomach didn't have time to rebel before he heard Aram giggle again. He tried to turn, but the impact of a blow to the back of his head sent the world into a spiral of horrible, clawed monstrosities.

†††

Consciousness returned, and dragged in new, unpleasant friends.

95

Pat tasted sour, oily copper and assumed he'd vomited and somehow hit his mouth. He hadn't been this blackout-drunk since one time in college that had him swear off booze for a year. His head hurt, his stomach hurt, and so did everything else. For some reason, his face felt stiff and he couldn't open his eyes.

Pat tried to shift, and found he was sitting up. And that he was bound. With the realization returned his memories of the evening. Breath hissed through his nose, thick with the stink of vomit, blood and the same oily fish reek he'd smelled at the marina.

He'd have cursed himself for a fool, but he was too scared. Even without the monster he hoped he'd dreamed, Pat knew after years on the force what could happen when one person had another at their mercy like this.

"Oh, good. You're awake, Detective." The voice got closer as it spoke. Pat recognized Aram even with his eyes closed. "Ah, my friend's secretions have glued your eyes shut. Well, we can't have that. You need to see the truth." He barked a command in a language Pat didn't recognize. The strange words echoed inside his skull, driving spikes of nauseating pain through his already-abused brain.

The floor shuddered as something massive moved across it. Pat couldn't tell what it was until the smell of the monster struck him in the face. Its hideous presence suddenly loomed over him, and the churning reek of its breath sent cloying fingers deep into his lungs. His stomach roiled, threatening rebellion.

"Now, none of that, Detective Timmons," Aram counseled, his voice soft and unnaturally intense. "My kinsman from the deep is only going to help. I should encourage you, however, to hold very still. I don't genuinely care. You only need one eye, really."

With the implicit threat hanging in the air, Aram barked another command in that mind-shattering tongue. Afflicted with a sudden, bone-deep fear, Pat froze, barely breathing. The horrific abomination bent low, its noxious breath hissing between its fangs and wafting gently over Pat's face.

A flickering touch ghosted over his cheekbone. Something cold and wet. Pat's pulse drummed wildly in his ears, and it seemed as though every muscle in his body contracted into a rock-hard knot.

The chill touch, moist and worm-like, slid up his face and began to lave his eyes. He gripped the armrests in iron fingers. A rhythmic clack-clack sounded very near, in jarring counterpoint to his racing pulse. The obscenely intimate caress went on and on, until Pat was certain he was going to scream.

Then the menacing presence receded, taking the violating *something* and the clacking sound with it. Pat choked back a sob as his entire body shuddered with reaction. Saliva flooded his mouth and he swallowed convulsively, his throat quivering just on the point ejecting the contents of his abused stomach.

"Now then, Detective, that wasn't so bad, was it?" Aram's footsteps moved around from behind Pat. "You should be able to open your eyes freely, now that my kinsman has seen to you." And the bastard giggled.

Pat opened his eyes, and very nearly puked again. He'd didn't know what he'd expected, but it hadn't been a pit of hell. Unclean growths, like some kind of monstrous, dry-land barnacles, covered the walls and poured down to spill across parts of the floor. Gelid slime coated the things, obscuring hard edged shells without softening them. Near where the thing from the marina stood, the growths clattered, shells pulsing and rubbing. Long, feathery spindles licked at the air, and contributed to the effluvium with spurts of gaseous vapor.

The crustaceous eel-man squatted over a mass of the things. Its head weaved back and forth, muzzle agape. It inhaled the gas from the shells, and as it did, a pale nictitating lid slid over its dead, black eyes. Dangling from its mouth writhed a tentacular member the color of dead skin that twitched in time to the clack, clack of slime-laden shells. Pat shuddered and looked away.

Directly in front of him an odd design was carved into the floor. The lines seemed to melt and flow into and over each other in ways that defied reality. Here and there, symbols etched deep into stone flickered and danced to the pounding in Pat's head. Despite the difficulty he found seeing it, it was impossible to miss the shackles bolted to the floor. Light caught in more of the symbols carved around each restraint.

Just beyond the weird, circular carving, water lapped up a set of carved steps. The rainbow sheen of oil swirled across the amorphous surface. It was somehow hypnotic to Pat's tortured sense.

At last, he looked up at Aram. The young man had changed into a robe the color of rust, adorned with embroidery that matched the symbols carved into the design on the floor. The robe was open at the neck, revealing an odd necklace made of strips of brown leather and what looked like shiny, black crab-legs.

"Where's Carla?" Pat asked, his voice harsh with suppressed emotion and expressed stomach acid. "Was she even real?" Pat felt his anger surge; recognized the boiling stew of rage under his fear. He fed it, focusing on the betrayal and imprisonment instead of the madness-inspiring monstrosities around him.

"Oh, Carla's real enough. She's in another room down here. Don't worry, Detective: we're taking good care of her. She needs to be healthy for the ritual in the new moon next week. She will be blessed above all women, for she will bear the first of the New Ones." Aram's lips bent up in the same ghastly grin he'd shown before, and now Pat recognized what else was in his eyes. Despair, and gibbering insanity.

"Then what do you need me for?" He cleared his throat and spat at the younger man's feet. "Is your name even Aram Kazemi, you backstabbing son of a bitch?"

Aram's smile grew fixed, and sweat broke out on his forehead. The bastard's fingers flexed, and for a moment Pat thought he saw his chest twitch. Then he realized with horror that what he'd thought was a necklace was actually moving on its own.

"What the hell?" Pat couldn't hold back the explosion.

Aram came back to himself and stroked the thing draped across his chest.

"Oh, do you like this? I should think you'd want to. As to this-" he gestured toward his body, "-this host is Aram, whose girlfriend resides at our pleasure and insistence a short ways away." The light of madness in his eyes grew stronger, and Pat wouldn't have been at all surprised to see them start glowing in truth. "But for *me*, I am *Iaphneth;* one of the Created. I am grown for the Mother's service. And-"

He was interrupted by a hissing roar from the creature at the other side of the room. It had bolted upright and stood swaying, clicking its claws together.

"Ahh, just what we were all waiting for," Aram- no, *Iaphneth* gloated, his face taking on a cast of infernal glee. "You, most especially, honored Detective. Watch!"

And Pat watched, unable to look away. The clacking of shell on shell from the things on the floor increased in tempo to a rattling hum that penetrated the mind and settled into the empty places of the heart. Brilliant crimson feathers whipped out, lashing the air now in orgiastic fury.

Pat's pulse raced, cold sweat beading on his forehead to drip into his eyes. He felt caught between terror and a perverse excitement, and his Catholic soul rebelled. Distantly, he heard a sound, as of stone rubbing together. He realized his jaws were clenched so hard his teeth ground.

With silence so abrupt it was painful, the thunderous rattle stopped. And with it, the violent motion of the virulently red-frilled tendrils, which disappeared into slime-covered shells as though they'd never been. All but one. That one remained, and its shell twitched. It came to Pat that he was witnessing the hideous birth of some inhuman horror, and his gorge rose.

Purple-black shell cracked with tiny detonations, and the bright red spindle collapsed to lay limp and twitching over the other eggs. More pops and crackles echoed through the chamber, their only competition the wheezing hiss of the monster and Pat's own strangled breathing.

And one other note. A moaning croon.

Pat looked over at Aram-*Iaphneth* and his guts twisted in shock and revulsion. The man's robe had fallen farther open, and the thing around his neck squirmed, waving tendrils and spidery claws toward the blasphemous nativity. Aram - or the kid's mouth, at least - crooned, stroking the thing that controlled his body with gentle caresses.

The crustaceous monster hissed, loud in the hushed room, and Pat whipped his head back around. The egg structure had shattered, releasing a cloud of putrid fog into the already fetid room. The mucoid sludge coating it held the shards together in a jagged, gelid mass. The eel-headed creature hovered over the rippling aggregation like nothing so much as a nervous parent, a parallel that made Pat shudder.

The remains of the egg heaved and pulsated with a wet, squelching gurgle. Pat was held fascinated, as finger-length legs the same red as the still quiescent tendril thrust out of the dark mess of mucus and shell fragments. At last, the foul thing dragged itself from its birthing chamber and lay on the floor, twitching weakly. Bright red legs and pale tentacles slowly darkened, all except for the original feathered whip-like appendage.

"Ahhh," Aram-*Iaphneth* sighed, the satisfaction in his/its voice profoundly disturbing. "Now, I think, Detective. It is time to introduce you to my - sibling." He turned and barked a phrase in that mind-bendingly wrong language, which set Pat's limbs twitching.

The horrible mutant picked up the now completely-darkened blend of insect and cephalopod, and stumped across the room toward Pat. His heart gave a lurch as the thing passed behind him, but he felt nothing. The hair on the back of his neck stood up, however, as Aram-*Iaphneth* turned to face him.

"The restraints should prevent you from hurting yourself, Detective. Or my fellow *Iaphneth*." Pat's mouth went bone-dry at his words, and he wrenched at the straps that bound him securely to the chair. "Oh, this will simply not do."

Snake-quick, Aram reached out and caught Pat's head in a grip of iron. Equally fast, his other hand caught Pat on the tip of the jaw, and his world went white. Through the sudden roaring in his ears, Pat heard Aram-*Iaphneth* growl something in the alien tongue, and his limbs twitched. It felt as though his entire body suffered the pins-and-needles of paresthesia at once.

Weight settled across Pat's shoulders, and a scrabbling sensation rippled down his chest. His panicked breath whistled through clenched teeth as he tried once more to pull himself from the binding grasp of the monster in human form.

Pat felt a sharp pain at the back of his neck, and tried to scream. His heartbeat raged as atavistic terror took control, but Pat was no longer in control.

"I am Iaphneth! Now you are MINE!"

He heard a far-off sound, and realized that it was *his* voice, but that he hadn't made it. The part of him that called itself "Pat" slid down into a nightmare of grasping claws in the dark, and horrible, obscene caresses.

†††

Pat came back to himself. Remembered terror made a hash of his thoughts, and for a moment, he didn't know where he was. Barely knew *who* he was. His heart still pounded a brutal tattoo in his chest. Breath rushed in and out of nostrils no longer clogged with the rank stench of alien abominations. The sun still rode in the sky, albeit for just a little longer that day.

His hands ached where they sat in his lap, one wrapped around the other. His jaw ached, and he deliberately stretched it from side to side until it popped. He quietly reveled in possessing the ability to perform even that small motion.

Pat remembered briefly - no flashback, this - that dark time under the *Iaphneth's* perverted domination. The malevolent intelligence used him to flout procedure, stomp on civil rights and go where a mere college student was unable.

All while Pat's consciousness had ridden in a cage of chitinous razored legs and groping, fleshy tentacles in the back of his own skull. It took serious effort to refrain from vomiting. Again.

He'd watched as the horrible thing used him to stalk a bouncer, memorizing his habits. He'd observed as it incited a riot using his face, and then sheathed his body in its viscid, clinging secretion and molded it into his father's face, which it picked it out of Pat's memory. His just-relaxed fists clenched again in sudden rage.

When he'd woken up in the hospital with Jaime passed out in the chair next to him, clear-headed for the first time in days, Pat had wept. He'd luxuriated in the erstwhile normal sensation of wiggling his toes. After Jaime had woken up and started asking questions, reality fell on Pat like the proverbial ton of bricks. He couldn't exactly tell his partner he hadn't been in touch because something from a nightmare had been running him like a marionette. Jaime hadn't liked the answer he'd had to give, and hated that Pat hadn't told him everything.

When the bouncer and his girlfriend - or not: he didn't think they were sure of their relationship - walked in the next day, he'd been able to tell them. After all, they'd seen what happened, knew it from experience. Mike had shown him the very coin now nestled in his palm, and described the night from his perspective.

Mike told him about Tourney and his one man crusade against shadow monsters in the underground, and through the courageous veteran, he'd met Melody and felt the power of her music. The park where she played, near the Flatiron Building, was one of the safest places in the city. He'd checked.

And now he'd met Vincent, who matched the descriptions Mike and Avi's friend Anne had given him of a violinist who'd been enthralled by some kind of parasitic intelligence in a nightclub that didn't exist. Anne directed him to a building in Soho, and a door that descended into an empty room. One that distinctly didn't lead into a forest as she'd described.

Pat believed her, though.

He'd shown up for work, only to be put on administrative leave while Internal Affairs "checked into his activities" for the previous week or so. Whole portions of which weren't actually in his memories. Locked in terror in his own mind, Pat just couldn't remember a lot of what happened while the *Iaphneth* rode him. He had no idea where its lair was, for example.

He stared down at the coin, willing it to tell him its secrets. He knew the little object had some doozies. He could feel it, the same way he'd felt drawn to Vincent's battle. He knew it was a battle, even if the kid wouldn't tell him anything. Yet. They'd talk again, Pat knew. Dr. Thomas - Will, who as a student had volunteered in an after-school choir at Pat's church - would make sure he got a chance to talk to Vincent again.

"You've got something for me," he told the little gold coin with the worn, smiling face on one side. The little disc, smaller and thicker than a dime, beat against his raw-worn senses.

That was the other thing he'd gained. A blessing, though Father

Morelli at Saint Andrew's might not look at it that way. God knows, Pat would have given it back to erase the last several days. He knew Vincent lived up a floor, not just because he'd mentioned it on the drive, but because Pat could feel him up there. He radiated energy, in a way Pat hadn't felt before the *Iaphneth*.

Certain people had always felt more, well, present than others, but he'd never thought that might be anything spiritual. Too much like the magic in Granddad's stories. He'd felt it with Mike, Tourney, and Melody, too, though in different ways. Given their stories, he was probably responding to the different ways their gifts worked.

He stared hard at the coin in his hand. Vincent passed it to him right before he'd opened the car door, his face inscrutable. Relief flooded his thin face once Pat closed his fingers around it, and he'd actually looked like a seventeen-year-old kid for the first time.

Pat felt the thing in his hand. There was a weight there, a mass, that had nothing to do with the physical world. It worried him. The sense of leashed might was similar to the one he'd experienced the first time he held a gun. Here was something potentially very dangerous. Only this time, he didn't know how to pull the trigger.

Pat turned around and looked at his new rod. His previous one had disappeared from where he'd seen it last. Of course, the other *Iaphneth* could have taken it, but he suspected it had just fallen prey to the Big Apple's homeless population. He could think of worse things. He made up his mind.

Pat drove back to Chelsea. He'd start looking there.

✝✝✝

The walk from the parking complex gave him time to think. He should have been sleeping, but that was dangerous. Nightmares were nearly constant since he'd woken up without the thing on him. He'd asked Mike about it, thinking the healer had missed something, but Tourney been able to help the most. The cagey veteran told him about his struggles with PTSD, suggesting Pat look into counseling. He'd met guys on the force who'd developed it, but never figured himself for it.

Pat's newly developed mystical radar pinged him a block before he got to the park. His heart-rate sped up dramatically, and he started

103

scanning his surroundings. He wished he had a weapon beyond the pole in his hand. Even that was cased, broken down into sections.

When he got to the park proper, Pat saw the source of the odd sensation. Melody sat under a tree, playing a penny whistle instead of her usual violin. Despite the late hour, a small crowd had gathered, and the hat on the ground in front of the young musician nearly overflowed with loose change, and no few bills.

Pat slouched over toward her. Pat saw when she noticed him, and returned her nod. He'd gotten the impression she didn't really trust him. To be fair, he supposed, most New Yorkers probably didn't really trust the police. He usually didn't, and he *was* the police. But that just meant she must have something important to tell him.

Or something she thought was important, which wasn't necessarily the same thing, as he knew from experience. The spritely notes of her whistle worked her peculiar magic on the crowd. People dragging from one place to another perked up.

He could feel it himself, quite apart from the way her abilities seemed to rasp on his still-raw spirit. He waited - not terribly patiently - while she finished her song. He tried to lose himself in the music. The pain and the way her fingers flickered with sparks of golden magic nobody else seemed to see detracted, though. When the song ended, Pat shuddered, only then realizing how discomforting the use of magic was.

"Thank you, all," Melody said in her quiet soprano voice. "Please, be safe tonight."

She'd told Pat a little of her story, and he was - quite frankly - astonished at her fortitude. True, she rarely smiled, but with a dead father and a barely-functional mother, that made sense. Quite apart from what she'd witnessed all her adult life.

It wasn't great fun to wonder if you were just plain nuts.

The crowd dispersed, behaving in ways strange to the police officer. They smiled at each other; they wished each other safe travels and a good night. Unusual, in Pat's experience, outside of New Year's Eve and bare handful of other occasions. Melody moved out from under the tree, into the pool of light cast by a lamppost. Pat saw she went barefoot. She'd done that at the other park, as well.

"Detective Timmons, I thought I'd find you here." Melody Devreux's serious demeanor gave her an uncommon maturity for one of her relative youth. She didn't look Pat in the eyes, which was unfortunate. She had some of the bluest eyes Pat remembered seeing. Or it was just everything before a few days ago felt wan and gray somehow. Besides, he had no business with any woman, let alone one just out of legally actionable territory.

Pat shook himself. The least little thing seemed to make him lose focus, and that led to trying to push out with his painful, new senses. Testing his surroundings with mental fingers in a way he'd long since internalized with his strictly mundane abilities.

"Miss Devreax, I hadn't expected to see you, at all, tonight." Pat scanned their surroundings. People wandered as they were wont: a couple walked arm-in-arm through along the waterside, a jogger passed them up, a group of youngsters laughed and joked farther into the park. "Please, call me Pat. I have no idea how long I'll get to keep the title."

"I'm not surprised, Patrick -," ever formal, even using a given name, "- but you'll need me tonight, where you're going."

"And where am I going tonight?" Pat forced his tone smooth. Everything supernatural bothered him. All the cops he knew had some kind of superstition - he himself kept a hand-forged iron nail in his pocket thanks his Granddad - but seeing the worst parts spring to horrible life still set him very much on edge.

"It's the new moon tonight, and you're going to find Carla." Pat didn't miss the way her knuckles whitened where her hands gripped the black-enameled whistle.

"I'm going to look for where that thing took me," Pat corrected, forcing the words through the sudden tightness in his chest. The denial fell flat. He'd *been* looking, ever since the hospital discharged him. He'd managed to contact Tourney again, who'd had no luck. Studying and bouncing kept Runey busy, and Anne Cavanaugh's schedule didn't allow for a lot of extracurricular activities. Vincent was, well, Pat wasn't sure about Vincent yet. He was pretty certain Vincent wasn't sure of Vincent yet, either.

"And I can help you," she said, her voice low with intensity.

"And I *have* to be there."

Pat kept his hands at his sides, despite an urge to stuff them into his pockets like a recalcitrant schoolboy. All the reasons she shouldn't come sprang to his lips. Then, she looked him in the eye, and the expression in her cobalt eyes silenced him. Her fear - and dogged determination - beat on him.

"How - how do you know?" Pat wasn't sure why he asked. His scalp tightened as his emotions responded to hers. He wanted to hunch his shoulders against an unfelt wind. His mind reeled as if massive, unseen things moved close at hand.

Melody tipped her face down so it was in shadow, her intensely blue eyes no longer skewering him with the force of her intentions. Pat felt shaken, and was shocked to realize he'd somehow jammed one hand into a pocket, where it was clenched around the suspicious gold coin.

"I felt it tonight, while I was playing. Right before you arrived." She tossed her head, sending glossy chestnut hair flaring. She scowled, which set Pat aback before he realized she hadn't aimed it at him. "It just came to me; I'm not sure why. I knew you'd be going to look for those monsters and I knew you'd need me to come along."

"Um."

She nodded in agreement, then bent down to slip her shoes back on.

"Is that - new?"

She nodded again, and when she looked up at him, her face was worried.

"I don't think any of us are exactly used to this, this whatever it is," she said.

Pat's lips twisted into a wry smile.

"Yeah, well. It's a hell of thing, when nightmares become real and you can do things you never thought possible. I'm not really sure I want to live in this new world, you know?"

Melody nodded, the strength of the motion shaking her entire slim form.

A thought occurred to Pat.

"If you only got this message just now, what were you doing

here tonight in the first place?"

Melody's pale face went the steely blank of furious anger. Pat unconsciously tensed in reaction. He'd seen that look before on people who were about to go berserk.

"I lost a regular."

Pat blinked, lost in the sudden switch.

"I'm - sorry?"

Melody turned her scowl on him.

"I've been playing in parks for weeks now, and I've gotten to recognize some of the people who are usually there at certain times. Patterns, flows, the way people fall into routines." She shot him an irritated look.

Pat nodded. He did, indeed, know how people fell into patterns of behavior. It was human nature: take the same bus to work at the same time. Wear the same clothes on the same days. With few exceptions, most people even ate the same dishes for most of their lives.

"One lady comes by Washington Square Park every morning and listens to me play a few songs. I think she works for the university. She always looks sad, but she's been staying longer and longer over the last couple of weeks, and seems like she's, well, getting happier."

Her mouth worked, and her breath whistled in and out her nose. "This morning, she walked past. I called her name, and when she didn't respond, I called again. She usually wears open-necked shirts -" the hair on the back of Pat's neck stood up, "- and always with a specific necklace: a piece of deep green jade."

"And today, she wasn't." Pat stared into nothing. "She was wearing a loose, button down shirt, or a bulky sweater, or a coat with a high collar. And she probably works late, outside of normal business hours, at least." The coin's uneven edge bit into Pat's palm. "She walked home, or to the subway, or to a bus station. And there was a young man who just needed a moment of her time -"

"Patrick!"

Melody's strangled cry wrenched Pat back to himself. He shook like the proverbial leaf. Tension racked his entire body, driven by a potent concoction of remembered terror and blinding rage. Melody's wide eyes acted on him like a chill rain, cooling the red fury that gripped him.

"I'm sorry."

She looked hard at him, harder than a woman that many years his junior should be able to.

"Mike was right: there's something damaged in you, Detective."

Pat stared at her, unable to speak. Runey'd told him much the same thing when he woke up in the hospital. A stew of thoughts and emotions seethed just inside his skin, and under it all was a terrible dread.

"We spoke before you visited me," she continued. "When he healed you, he saw what he called gray places. Something in you that wasn't physical, but was affected. By what you experienced."

Pat shuddered. It fit. He wanted to lash out. At Melody. At the world. Trauma did things, and he'd found little more traumatic than being reduced to a passenger in your own body by something so unquestionably evil.

"I'm troubled by your drive to resolve this." She shook her head as Pat's eyebrows climbed. "Not ending the threat and finding Carla, but that it be you and now. Why do you need to be the one to do this, when by rights you should be healing still?"

"I can find them," Pat grated, his jaw still tight with inner turmoil.

Melody blinked, confused.

"I - I can feel. Things," he elaborated, forcing words through suddenly stiff lips. "I knew you were here in the park long before I heard your pipe. I could tell you were playing." He shook his head, at a loss. "I don't know how to describe it. I just knew."

She crossed her arms and tapped her chin with the whistle.

"As though somebody stood behind you, whispering it into your ear?" Her eyes turned opaque, as though she was looking into another place.

"No, not at all." He shook his head. "It was more like hot, summer sun on a patch of sunburn, and about as pleasant. I know about where I'm going by where it hurts." Just like he'd known where to find Vincent, and when Mike was trying to heal him.

"That's - not -" Melody cut off.

"Not the same as the rest of you," Pat asked. He shook his head, staring over her head. He pulled his hand out of his pocket and showed her the coin nestled in his palm. Melody's eyes narrowed in sudden speculation as he continued. "No, not really, is it? Which makes sense, considering I just got handing this a little bit ago by somebody who has no reason to know the rest of us. And I haven't felt anything like the rest of you described. On the other hand, this - *sense* - does mean I should have a fool-proof way to find -" his lips twisted in a silent snarl, "- *them*, doesn't it?"

Melody didn't answer, and for a moment they both stared at the shiny disc in his hand. Melody reached out and closed his fingers around the coin, a gentle touch that surprised Pat.

"And so it has to be you."

"But it doesn't have to be you, too," he objected, still troubled with the idea of taking an untrained young woman into harm's way. Pat was certain she didn't actually want to come. Or at least, she was afraid of what she'd find if she did. Which he could respect: he knew what there was to find, and was pretty scared already.

"Yes, it does have to be me," she said, voice firm. She looked him in the eyes again, and again he was struck by the iron determination in hers. "If only because I won't tell you where I followed my regular, Naomi, to when she left work."

Pat's jaw dropped.

"What? What do you mean, *won't tell me*?" Incandescent fury seared Pat's mind.

She gave him a cool look he couldn't help but admire.

"I think it's obvious, Detective. If you don't agree to my accompanying you tonight, I won't tell you what I know. It's the new moon tonight, as I'm sure you've noticed, which doesn't leave a whole lot of time."

Pat's head throbbed.

"I'll -"

"You'll do nothing but agree to let me come along. To do anything else, anything to force my compliance would compromise your honor as a police officer." She cocked her head sideways.

"Wouldn't it?"

Pat glared at her. He wasn't a big man, but he had to have a good forty or fifty pounds on Melody, as well as a decade more life experience. And she stood there dictating terms. And she was right, dammit! Pat knew he wouldn't wring her neck, as much as she might deserve it. He couldn't do a damn thing without turning into the thing the monster had made of him. And she knew it just as well as he did.

"Fine," he growled after a moment.

At his grudging acquiescence, a tension he hadn't noticed drained from her. The skin around her eyes and mouth loosened and her shoulders slumped. When she took a deep, shuddering breath, and let it out again, Pat realized how scared she'd been. And still was, unless he missed his guess completely.

"But," he continued, "you do what I say. If I say run, you run. If I say hide, you find the deepest hole you can and pull it in after you. If I say jump -"

"I ask how high on the way up?" She assayed a small smile, which transformed her face.

"Damn right, you do." He looked around, and tentatively felt the surrounding area with his still tender senses. Low-grade nausea immediately burned in his gut, but he didn't feel anything but the usual amount of spiritual noise. It was the same misery he'd been picking up on all his life, though he didn't really know it. Committed, he bent down to retrieve his fishing gear.

"Well, you're the one with the information."

She looked at him, cobalt eyes widening a hair.

"You don't need anything, Patrick? A gun or something?"

He looked down at the case in his hand.

"I'll need to stop by the parking garage where my car lives to drop this off, but that's it."

It was a quick trip to the garage, and they made it in silence. Melody didn't seem to have anything to say - Pat was impressed she'd spoken as much as she had - and he was too preoccupied. He kept pushing at his newfound senses, like an athlete testing an injury. He was pretty sure he was going to develop a tic, since he winced every time he did.

After that, Melody quickly led him to a place every New Yorker knew.

"Times Square?" Incredulity colored his question. She nodded, her blush showing despite the variegated color of the square by night. He looked around, watched the hundreds of people moving through the square, never mind the time of day. Tracking anybody through the busiest intersection of the busiest city in the world was a nightmare under the best of circumstances, and he said so.

Melody just shook her head.

"Naomi didn't stop here," she said, and began walking, with a native's disregard for traffic. Pat stuck to her, keeping his head up as she led him through the pedestrian mall along Broadway and then down the stairs to the subway station.

At first, Pat thought crowd noise started his head pounding. A lot of people generated a lot of sound, but there was something else involved. The hair on the back of his neck stood up, and the skin across his forehead felt tight. They scanned their passes and slid through the turnstiles, and Pat snagged Melody's elbow and pulled her out of the flow of traffic.

She cast him an oblique look, but obliged when he gestured. The slow throb in his head was uncomfortable, but not greatly painful. Pat pushed at his surroundings with his senses and nearly jumped out of his shoes. His feet suddenly felt on flame. He damped his ability with a grimace. When Melody looked a question, he leaned close enough to be heard over the press of humanity.

"Well, something's down there, underneath us."

Her expression showed she understood, and she motioned him to follow her again. Once they were on the platform, she pointed off to one side.

"Naomi went over there, then disappeared. I waited for a while, but she didn't come back."

Then Pat took the lead, walking over to the spot Melody indicated. He turned around and surveyed the platform with a practiced eye. When Melody made as if to keep going, he shook his head, and then walked over to a bench. Melody followed, her expression one of puzzlement. He sat down next to the homeless man, there, a grizzled man wearing a faded parka in olive drab.

"I bet you see a bunch of stuff."

The man started, and then his eyes narrowed.

"I ain't telling you nothing, cop."

Pat smiled, in his element.

"Yeah, I'm a cop. So what?" He reached into the coin pocket of his jeans and pulled out a folded twenty. He made sure the man saw the number. "I just want to know one thing, man. You in?"

Suspicion showed clearly on the street dweller's face, joined by a rising anger. Melody, who'd been leaning against the wall on Pat's other side, poked her head around.

"Do you know Tourney Martin?"

Pat blinked at the apparent non-sequitur, but the homeless man's face broke into a grin.

"Sure, I know Tourn! He keeps us all safe, down below." His face crumpled. "Mostly. As much as he can." He cast a ferocious scowl at the people waiting for the next train. "They don't know it, but there's bad things in the dark."

Pat nodded. He knew what evil lurked in the heart of the city.

"We're helping Tourney," Melody said, her soprano voice cutting clearly through the noise of the platform. The man transferred his masterful scowl to Pat, his suspicion back in spades. Melody opened her mouth again, but Pat waved her quiet.

"Have you seen him spin his sword?"

The man's bright green eyes disappeared widened. It was quite a sight to see his bushy, gray eyebrows disappear into the rat's nest of wiry hair sticking out from under the grubby cap he wore.

"You seen that?" The man asked, amazement lighting up his face. "He let you? Craziest thing I ever saw, that was. We was down in the dark, and a thing with arms long as you, Missy, trying to carry me off! I was so scared I pissed myself! Usually the things I see ain't actually there. Can't touch me, leastwise. All of a sudden, Tourn shows up, waving that peacemaker of his around. I've seen it before, but this time, wow! It was lit up gold like one in a church somewheres."

"Yeah, I've seen it," Pat said, his voice haunted. He'd seen it from the other side. It looked like the sword of God, come to avenge. He'd prayed it would end the torture his life had become, and instead it freed him. He prayed he'd be able to get some back from those horrible things.

"Yeah, well Tourn whipped that thing around, and next thing you know I'm sitting on the floor with a big, black arm turning into goo on my pants." He mimed the action as he narrated. The man's garrulous enthusiasm carried him on through the end of his brief story. "Wowwee, what a stink, but at least it covered up the smell of the piss, begging your pardon, Missy."

Melody waved his apology away with one hand, her other covering what Pat suspected might be a smile. The old fellow certainly was a character.

"We're just looking to find out if you saw a lady come through here earlier," Pat said.

"Might have done. I've seen lots of ladies come through here."

"This one was about Patrick's age," Melody said, gesturing to Pat. "She has light brown skin, black eyes and hair. She had her hair up, and a jacket that stopped about here." She gestured to the bottom of her ribcage. "But the collar came up to under her chin. She'd have walked through her and around there," she pointed around the bend of the wall.

The old man shuddered.

"Her." His voice went flat, and his face blank. "Yeah. I saw her. She gave me a look to freeze the blood in your veins. And her coat moved." His jaw worked and he spat on the concrete floor, earning a black look from a passerby. "Not like the wind was blowing it. Like there was something moving around *underneath* the coat."

Pet felt his stomach clench.

"Did she come back?" Melody asked in a voice hard enough to shave stone.

"No. I ain't seen her come back through here. Might have somewheres else, though," he added. Pat didn't think so. With the night of the full moon upon them, he suspected any other *Iaphneths* to have returned to the fold, so to speak. He passed the twenty to the grim-faced man.

"Thanks for your help."

"Yeah, no problem." He looked at Pat, and a sharpness flashed into his eyes. "When you see him, you tell Tourney that Sergeant Murphy says to watch his six, y'hear?" In an instant, decades of rough wear dropped away, and Pat clearly saw the Marine that Murphy used to be.

"Will do, Sergeant," he said. "And should you find anything you think we should know about, you can send it care of Detective Patrick Timmons."

"Please come by Washington Square or Madison Square Park sometime and hear me play."

Murphy looked up at her, his face unreadable.

"I might just do that, Missy. Look after yourself. And the cop."

Murphy heaved himself to his feet and moved quietly into the crowd, which swallowed him in an instant. Pat looked after him for a moment, then shook his head.

"Shall we?"

Melody met his gaze with her blue one, eyes shining with unshed tears.

"How do we let people get that way, Patrick?"

He shrugged.

"It's not usually about *let*," he said, standing up. "For most in the sergeant's situation, they've chosen to live outside society, and the best we can do is show them kindness every now and again. As much as they'll accept."

He stood, watching the press and surge of humanity moving around them for just a moment. Normal people, moving about their normal lives, just of pain, misery, drudgery and hopefully just enough joy to get them through the day. And they had no idea what horrors lurked under their normal, everyday feet.

But he did.

"Last chance to back out, Missy," he offered, using Murphy's nickname for her. "Stay safe; maybe live to fight another day."

Pat looked to Melody, meeting her once more steely gaze with his own. Her spine was straight, like the will that drove it, and he knew she wouldn't quit. It was no surprise when she shook her head.

"All right, then. Let's do this." He stepped around the corner.

To see a closed maintenance door. Melody reached for the doorknob, a lever in industrial steel, but Pat put out a hand to stop her. Something was stuck in the keyhole, as though someone had forced melted wax out from the inside of the mechanism, to ooze down the handle. If wax was a translucent pale purple. He leaned close and sniffed. The usual odors of humanity, as well as the antiseptic bite of chlorine bleach. Layered over it, though, a thread of oily fish and the something alien that told him they were, indeed, on the right track.

With nothing else to indicate caution, Pat pushed gently on the lever. With a sharp crack, a fat, blue spark popped in the safety light mounted over door frame. Evidently, somebody or some*thing* had messed with the mechanisms the Metro Transit Authority usually used to keep people out of its private domains. Though he noted with wry amusement that that Keep Out sign had actually been wiped clean of the usual coat of grime.

When Pat pushed, the door stuck. With a grimace, he pushed harder, and when it became obvious even that wasn't going to be enough, he threw his shoulder into it. With a juicy pop, the door came loose and swung inward, and Pat and Melody caught a billow of stench in the face. Pat swore and spat, while Melody whirled and vomited.

Hardened slime coated the door jamb, and oozed down to form a puddled mass of sludge on the floor. Pat swallowed convulsively, and turned to Melody, placing a hand on her shoulder to steady the shaking young woman.

"You okay?"

She straightened with a jerk, and threw an alarmed look over her shoulder. Pat removed his hand, a little unsure of himself. Then Melody relaxed, and her expression turned apologetic. She gave him a wan smile before speaking.

"That's - nasty." She spat, and pulled a white handkerchief from her pocket to wipe her mouth. Pat was surprised. He didn't think people carried them anymore.

"Yeah, and there's worse to come," Pat said. "Take a minute out here while I look inside."

Melody nodded, eyes still watering, and Pat stepped over the puddle of gook on the floor. The stuff coated the inside of the door, as well as the jamb and a good portion of the walls around the it. The stuff froze the light switch in the up position, but the fluorescent bulbs flickered.

Pat took a careful breath, but with the door open, simple airflow seemed to be enough to clear out most of the foul odor. He looked around the little room.

Another doorway stood opposite and offset a few feet, though it was just a black hole. The door seemed to be missing completely. Some cleaning supplies lay in one corner, next to an industrial sink and a metal cabinet.

He crossed to the cabinet and gingerly opened the door. When nasty alien monster things failed to leap out at him, he took a closer look. More cleaning supplies. A sound behind him brought his head around to see Melody easing her way inside.

"Careful with the stuff on the floor; it's bound to be slick." At her nod, he went back to examining the room. The flickering of the lights didn't make that particularly easy, and after a moment he judged that there just wasn't much to see. Pat slipped to the darkened doorway, and noticed that the door had been wrenched off, leaving tortured hinges behind. Remembering the monstrous creature that likely waited below, he didn't think that would have been hard to manage.

After a short moment, Pat found his eyes adjusting to the dim light. And the space was lit, despite its appearance in the other room. The room - much larger than the entry - contained several large machines, fenced off with a sign warning of electrocution danger. The gate appeared to have been forcibly removed, probably by the same chitinous horror. A heavy extension cord with danger yellow insulation stood out of a large socket on the wall near one of the machines, and ran out the open gate and down an open hatch in the floor. A hatch from which spilled the dim light in the room.

Pat reached into his jacket and drew his pistol, just as Melody stepped through the doorway. The M1911 had been a gift from his father, who'd used it in Vietnam to good effect. Pat had replaced several parts of it, to include substituting a threaded barrel. Which was necessary for the suppressor he drew from the right side of his shoulder rig. The sound of metal on metal as he screwed the one to the other drew his companion's attention, and when Melody realized what he held, she gasped.

"What-?"

Pat lowered the pistol and held his finger to his lips. Leaning close he spoke calmly.

"Our next move is through there," he pointed to the open hatch, "and neither of us knows what's down there, though I've got a couple of ideas. While I'd like to find Carla and simply disappear, I don't think that's likely. This is the only way I can think of evening the odds. Though I'd appreciate it if you didn't mention it to anybody."

It wasn't that the gun was illegal. The suppressor, either. He even had all the proper permits. Though since they'd been signed by his superiors in the NYPD and he fully expected his membership in that august body to cease any time, it might be better that nobody got word he was carrying a .45 in his "off time."

Melody gave him a look pregnant with interest, her eyes luminous in the artificial twilight, but managed to stifle her curiosity. She shrugged, and gestured toward the hatch. He nodded, and moved toward it.

"Wait," Melody hissed.

When Pat turned to look, she'd ducked back into the entryway, and scooped up the mop lying on the floor. She shoved at the slimed door, pushing it closed. The coating showed obvious cracks, but only for a moment. Before Pat's eyes, the stuff flowed together, leaving a rippled sheet of transparent goop across the door. He cocked his head as Melody rejoined him.

"I didn't want anybody else to stumble in here by accident," she apologized.

Pat shrugged. He just didn't want to get caught where he shouldn't be. He knelt at the edge of the hole in the floor, and peered down into the next room. Which was exactly like the one they were in, with just a bit better lighting. Someone had set up a cot in one corner with some blankets on it, and a utility light hung from a bracket on the wall.

Irritated, Pat unscrewed the suppressor from his pistol, and slid them both into his rig before climbing down the ladder as quietly as he could. He was just reattaching them when Melody joined him. The look she gave him combined equal parts amusement, questioning and apprehension, and she flicked a glance at the gun. He frowned and jerked a shoulder in a violent half shrug.

Taking a deep breath, Pat pushed tentatively at the part of his being torn open by his recent enslavement. Immediately his gut churned, shooting flickers of burning pain up his torso. He grunted, as external stimulus flooded over him. The sense of searing heat beat on his skin, even through his clothing, and carried with it a flavor of *wrongness,* as though a diseased sun shone on him. His eyes flickered closed as he tried to figure out the source.

When they'd been upstairs in the active part of the subway station, he'd felt it through the soles of his feet. Now that they were down a level, it had shifted. Now Pat felt it on his chest and legs, though not on his face.

"Down, still, I think," he gritted through clenched teeth. "And in front of us." Pat pulled back, and the roiling in his stomach subsided, but he still felt weak from the exercise. He opened his eyes to find himself on his knees, though he had no memory of how he'd gotten there.

Melody stared at him, her azure eyes full of concern and no small amount of fear.

"Patrick, you can't keep doing that. You turn white as a sheet every time." She put out a hand to help him up, but he waved her off. Her lips tightened, but she stood back as he heaved himself to his feet.

"The way I see it, we don't have much choice, and Carla has absolutely none." Pat stretched his jaw, which had clenched tight against the pain. Melody pursed her lips and shook her head, but didn't contradict him. He knew he was right, but devoutly wished for a better way.

Now that they were closer, he could actually feel whatever it was a bit, even while he wasn't actively trying to. It was the same wind-on-sunburn sensation he'd experienced at the park, but with that added texture that screamed poison.

After a moment, he felt solid enough to move on. He jerked his head and started forward, moving through the open doorway into a small supply closet like the one above. This one had neither supplies, nor a thick coating of slime over the door. Someone had duct-taped plastic strips full of LEDs at about head-height on the walls to give light. The power cords ran to a strip on the floor and back into the other room. Idly, Pat wondered who was footing the bill.

Pat stared at the closed door while Melody waited patiently. He didn't want to burst in on anybody. Stealth was their greatest advantage at the moment, and he was loathe to give it up. He was also distinctly unenthused about going through the door without any back-up but an untrained, unarmed nineteen-year-old.

Pat took a deep breath and reached for the door handle. He was surprised when Melody beat him to it. She stood to the inside of the door and looked a question at him. He castigated himself for not thinking of it first, and stepped back and nodded.

She opened the door, just a crack at first. The hinges neither squealed nor stuck, telling him somebody kept them well oiled. Pat saw next to nothing through the opening, and motioned her to open it wider. As she did, he scanned the space beyond. It looked like the mirror image of the station above, except for the flickering of reflected light on rippling water where tracks should be. Water, thick with scum and flotsam, which lapped against the rails in the bottom of the tunnel. The rails, he saw when he looked closer, had never been attached to the brackets that jutted, rust-covered and jagged out of the sluggish water.

Pat stepped up to the now-open door and saw that, at least for the curve the door opened onto, there was nobody in sight. He motioned to Melody who followed him out and into an eerie reflection of the busy station above. Down here the walls were covered with the graffiti of long-gone urban explorers. Kids, generally, who liked to wander around the unoccupied buildings and abandoned parts of the city. They'd driven him to distraction when he was a beat cop, and now he was basically one of them.

Pat crept along, scanning constantly for anything alive. Or anything dead, for that matter. He had no idea what - besides Aram, his monster, Naomi, and Carla - might actually be down here waiting for them. The taking of Melody's regular suggested the *Iaphneth* had been busy in the time since it had taken Pat, and he was willing to bet the creature had acquired more minions like he'd been.

The powerful stink of the monster's goop hung heavy in the air as they moved through the not-so-abandoned station, following the line of safety-lights. Farther along, they saw why: the large doors that presumably opened onto stairs to the next level had been sealed with chains and a large padlock, and then covered over in a thick layer of the disgusting sludge.

"Should we open that?" Melody leaned close enough for Pat to feel her breath on his ear as she spoke.

"No way." He shook his head. "Somebody from the MTA put the lock there, and it's a safe bet there's another door at the top of the stairs with another lock on it. There's a reason these things covered the doors with that nasty stuff." It would complicate their escape to have to go back up the ladder. Maybe closing the door upstairs hadn't been the best choice.

The pools of light led them through a darkness choked with the smells of the alien monster, but also of brackish seawater and dirt. The recent weather had done a real number on the abandoned station. In point of fact, Pat was having to pay no small amount of attention to placing his feet. The flooding had left mounds of blackish silt all over, including halfway up the walls. Someone had taken the time to clear a path in the clinging, slippery stuff, but the whoever it was had done at best a half the job.

They walked - crept, really - through the isolated pools cast by the hanging lamps. Melody moved with barely a whisper of cloth, but Pat felt as though his footfalls rang loud in the still air. He began to hear muffled sound, as if a neighbor had the television turned up, but not loud enough to make out actual words.

Moving deeper into the station, they found bridges made of planks crossed the watery canals of the unfinished subway tunnel. Pat was surprised. The bridges were basically scaffolding stretched across the gaps between platforms. Planks over piping, but sturdy. Unease stirred at the amount of work that had gone into them.

The two of them crossed the makeshift bridges, every creak and groan drawing a wince. The sound he'd heard grew louder, and it wasn't long before he discerned a rhythm to it. Someone - several someones - were chanting in unison somewhere deeper in. Halfway through the station, Melody touched his elbow.

"I can hear chanting up ahead," she said, when he leaned in.

"I've been hearing it for a while," Pat confirmed. So the ritual had already started. That was distressing. At least one life hung in the balance. "We can't have much time."

†††

"No. No! Let me go! Please, noooo!" An accented female voice echoed weirdly in the tunnel, accompanied by a surge in the chanting. Pat could almost distinguish individual words, and recognized the cadences as the mind-twisting language the *Iaphneth* had used to command its monster. A craven part of him wanted to turn around and forget the mission.

Instead, they sped up as they followed the cleared path through the platform. At the other side, another pipe-and-board bridge dove down into the darkness of one of the incomplete tunnels. Pat swallowed, and thought he heard Melody whimper. When he looked over his shoulder, he easily read the terror in her face. He remembered her past, how creatures of living shadow preyed on those around her and finally attacked her.

Struck by a thought, Pat reached into his pocket and pulled out the heretofore unresponsive gold coin. He stared at it, and when nothing happened, he rapped it with the butt of his automatic. Melody blinked, still scared, but obviously curious about his actions.

"All right, you devious little bastard," he told the tiny, grinning face. He kept his voice low, but loud enough for Melody to listen in. "I'm doing all the right things, here. I'm helping Melody, I'm helping Vincent, I'm going after the *Iaphneths* to rescue Naomi -" Pat's conscious mind reeled; he barely believed what he was saying, "- and I'll even promise not to kill Aram, if I can manage it *and* I get to put a few rounds in his monster. You keep helping people, all over this city. Every time something truly bizarre occurs, you're there."

Melody stared at him as though he'd lost his mind, and Pat wasn't

121

sure she was far off. Except that he'd been through hell in the not-so-distant past, and his common-sense incredulity had been strained well past the breaking point. He was nearly ready to believe in anything, God help him.

"Monstrous things out of nightmares, creatures that occupy bodies and move them around while the person's still inside, screaming with no voice?" All the tension, all the terror and fury, all the relief and shame he'd had no way to voice pushed his words out in a tumbled rush. "Now I need you - *we* need you, and Carla needs your help. The only edge I've got hits me with crippling pain and nausea, and Melody has zero training for this." As though he did. "I can't do this with what I have. *Please*," Pat begged. A distant, detached part of his mind noted his gun hand trembled.

A moment of pregnant silence descended as Pat finished. Coincidentally, even the formless, dreadful chanting subsided. Pat felt Melody's hand on his shoulder, offering what support she could. He kept his eyes on the tiny disc in his hand, willing *some*thing to happen.

The moment passed, and Pat felt a crushing wave of disappointment wash through him. He'd been wrong. He pushed with his odd, sick senses. Just slightly, the feathery, hesitant touch of a man testing an injury. He had to be sure.

Immediately, the nausea set Pat's stomach seething. He felt the mass of horrible wrongness ahead and below, burning on his skin. He felt Melody at his back. Waves of bright, vital energy drifted from her as she hummed a tune he hadn't heard until that moment. It still hurt, and he couldn't stifle a wince.

And from the damnably grinning little face -

A burst of brilliant golden illumination flashed from the coin. Melody's hand on his shoulder clenched with bruising force. For a split-second, Pat saw the bones in his hand. He should have been blinded, but wasn't.

Time seemed to slow down, and the wave of radiance rolled down the tunnel. The scaffolding on which they stood turned up ahead and dove into a ragged hole in the side of the tunnel. Melody's sotto voce hum transformed into a beautiful ballad he'd often heard in his regular pub. Somewhere close ahead, he heard the footfalls of something massive, and could tell it headed toward them.

More astonishing that his sudden sensitivity, was what the power from the coin - and there was far more there than met the eye - did inside him. He felt it surge up his arm from his hand, heat beyond heat that froze him where he stood for an endless instant. The consuming auric flames roared through his body in an exquisite agony, finally settling in his chest and head. Terrified wonder set his mind abuzz, at the sheer power inside his skin, at a force that could hold him stock still as the world seemed to shake around him.

Only good trigger discipline prevented Pat from firing a round into the tunnel wall. Even then, he felt his index finger curl with the force of his convulsion as his hands clenched into rock-hard knots. His head snapped back, and beams of brilliant golden light shone from his wide eyes and gaping mouth, clearly illuminating the tunnel ceiling. The same beams lanced out from between his fingers, splashing the cold concrete walls with radiant pools.

Melody cried out and covered her eyes, wrenching away the hand she'd placed on his shoulder. For a brief, endless moment, Pat felt as though he hung suspended over some unimaginable chasm, touching nothing. He only felt the raging torrent of power locked in his body.

And then, as suddenly as it had come upon him, it disappeared. Pat felt again the rickety solidity of the scaffolding bridge under his feet. He could smell the old sewage and musty earth, the damp concrete and stagnant water of the abandoned subway station. Pat felt whole for the first time since he'd awoken bruised in body and soul on the stiff, antiseptic-smelling hospital bed.

He could even hear the heavy footsteps clearly moving toward them. A sound his recent baptism had driven clean from his mind. A sound that changed from the thud of massive foot on earth to the creak of wooden board taking the weight of something they weren't built to hold.

Pat's heart leapt into his throat. Time slowed again, but this time with the familiar molten-glass flow of adrenalized combat. A low hiss crept into his ears, and he knew the eel-headed arthropoidal monstrosity from his nightmares neared the broken mouth of the tunnel ahead.

Pat jammed the bizarre little coin back in his pocket. Then he whirled, and saw in an instant that even if they could both make it back to the abandoned platforms before the abomination saw them, they had nowhere to hide that the thing couldn't sniff them out. Trusting to some instinct he couldn't name, and hadn't possessed bare moments before, Pat reached out to Melody. He pulled her into a dim, shadowed space between two of the safety lights, and down, so they crouched in dark.

Melody tensed when he wrapped his arm around her shoulders, but even as close in height as they were, he still had a good thirty pounds on her. Their only hope lay in remaining undiscovered, and he slipped his free hand over her mouth, knowing that her song, which she'd continued through the light-show, would bring the horror to their poor hiding place.

She threw an elbow into his side, but froze as an enormous claw seized on the edge of the opening, easily crumbling the thick cement. And then the thing stepped into the light, and they both stopped breathing. It had grown, in size and in its hideous, alien appearance. Its chitinous armor plating seemed thicker than Pat's memories. Ridges, gnarls and spikes pushed out in all directions, and its massive claws hung nearly to the floor. He almost didn't believe it was the same creature, but the ridges of luminescent horn adorning its head matched the spots it had worn in their earlier encounter. The eyes, too, were the same dead black pits.

Pat's heart lurched in his chest. He was certain they were about to be torn limb from limb. He hoped, prayed, that the things wouldn't see them, but couldn't comprehend how it wouldn't. He stared at the horror, locked in place, *needing* to stay hidden. He glared at the hated thing with such fierce concentration that his very vision started to waver. It was though he saw through heat waves.

The horror swept its head in quick, serpentine arcs. Its jaw hung open and it gasped in quick, shallow breaths. With no tongue, it might be tasting with some other organ. It looked hesitant. Almost, confused. A moment passed. Then another.

In the background, Pat heard the chanting pick up again. Then, a voice he recognized shouted something in a language he wished he did not. The horror's head whipped around to face directly behind it, and hissed. Aram roared something again, and Pat was glad he was no closer to the source of those sanity-shredding words. As it was, his head throbbed at the sounds.

The horror turned its head back forward and stared again at the place Pat and Melody hid. With a last hissing roar, the thing slammed a claw into the edge of the tunnel, cracking the solid concrete. Then the monstrous creature turned around and stumped back the way it had come.

Pat remembered to breathe again, gulping air into grateful lungs. Melody jabbed her elbow into his side again, and turned her azure glare on him for good measure.

"Don't do that," she ordered, her voice low and intense.

"Don't do what?" Pat countered. "Save our lives? Your humming would have attracted its attention." He didn't know that, and felt guilty for latching onto it as an excuse.

"You don't know that," she said, as though she'd read his mind. "Don't stop me from singing," she elaborated. "It's the only thing keeping me on my feet right now."

Pat gave her a hard look in the twilit gloom. Melody was always pale, but now her skin appeared chalky. She breathed in short, choppy gasps, and stared at him with unnerving intensity. Not knowing he should do, Pat nodded.

"You can still head back."

Her head jerked back and forth. She wrapped her arms around her ribcage and squeezed.

"I told you, you need me here. That hasn't changed."

Pat shrugged, still unconvinced. He had no way to make her go back, though. As he turned away and they moved toward the ragged opening in the tunnel wall, Melody began singing again. He almost lost his footing as it struck him: her song didn't hurt anymore. He heard it, felt it, but the soft notes didn't excite the same slow burn in his gut they had bare moments earlier.

Pat knew he should be terrified - and part of him was, a bit - but he'd spent long enough as walking wounded that the absence of pain brightened his entire outlook. He simply reveled in feeling good. He wanted to dance, and quelled the urge to whirl Melody around. He settled for flashing a smile over his shoulder at her. Her eyes widened in response, and he started to think they might actually make it to see the sunrise.

The unholy chanting grew louder as they approached the hole clawed in the side of the tunnel. Pat looked at the spot where the monster hit the tunnel. Cracks radiated out from the point of impact, and powdered concrete dust drifted in the dank air. On the floor, furrows marred the opening, and Pat pointed them out. It would be easy to twist an ankle. Melody nodded, never ceasing her song.

They slipped into the rough-hewn tunnel side by side, to the unpleasant accompaniment of the ongoing ceremony. The garbled words didn't split Pat's skull the same way Aram's commands had, however, and he eyed his petite companion. Melody had drawn her penny-whistle from whatever pocket she kept it. She held it before her like some holy symbol, keeping her other hand on the rough wall. Pat silently resolved to do whatever he could to ensure her song continued.

They moved down the passage until they came to a doorway of hewn stone. The string of safety lamps ended there, with the last one hung to illuminate the door. At some point in the distant past, someone had carved a set of symbols that made Pat's eyes water. Except for four at the corner that read "1926." So much for the distant past.

Pressed for time as they were, Pat took a moment to snap a picture of the carved doorway. Assuming they lived through the night, it would almost certainly be useful.

They passed through the doorway into a small room constructed of sharp-edged, tight-fitting stones. Much like the doorway itself. The room was lit by a pairs of torches, to set to either side of the portal in which they stood. A stairway down opened in the middle of the room. Reliefs adorned the walls, hideous things of debauchery and human sacrifice. On both of the side walls, inhuman abominations much like the one presumably below them strode through cities of bizarre architecture toward a point over the staircase on the wall opposite Pat and Melody.

There, a carved globe of the earth formed the arch of the doorway down, and over it a stone sea monster of gargantuan proportions heaved itself from stone waves. A master had made the room, but he must have been mad. He'd perfectly captured ancient cruelty in the god-beast's grotesque face, the hunger as one of its many heads devoured a tiny human form. Pat shuddered.

The chanting, clearer than before, echoed up out of the stairwell. Pat took a deep breath pushed out with the senses he'd been given. The familiar wrongness welled up from below them, but the only thing Pat really sensed was the space around him, and then the stone that made up the walls. He pushed past those to a bewildering mix of substances that set his mind reeling. With a start, he pulled back, gasping for breath. Melody looked a question at him, but kept singing.

Once Pat got his breathing back under control, he tried again. He narrowed his focus, pushing downward. He sent his senses down the stairs, following the tunnel as it curved into a tight spiral. He gained confidence as he went, feeling how he could follow the empty space, and stop feeling at the point where his ethereal sense encountered the stone walls of the passage.

For about two full turns of the spiral. It was as though he'd hit a wall, and couldn't feel anything past it. Up to that point sense the fit of the stones in the floor and walls. He even felt the tracks in the dust, but at that point, his new sense of things faded out completely. It was like trying to stare through thick fog, or a soot blackened window. There was something past it, but he didn't know what.

Pat pulled back until all he knew was what he saw, smelled, heard. He took a deep breath and closed his eyes. With every bit of himself he could muster, Pat pushed at that obscuring barrier, to the point where his head throbbed with the effort. At last, he came back to himself, to find Melody shaking him.

He leaned against the stone door jamb sucking air. Sweat trickled down his face, and when he wiped at his nose, his hand came away red. Melody glared at him. Pat was making a habit of angering her.

He heaved himself off the jamb, and almost fell over as his vision of the world split and warped. After a brief moment, the double vision realigned. In its wake, a pounding thud took residence just behind Pat's eyes.

"Oops."

Melody nodded her agreement, eyes narrowing in irritation, and shifted her song to one slightly languid. Pat's sudden headache eased slightly, and he smiled his thanks before walking down the stairs. She followed tight on his heels.

As they moved downward, the echoing chant grew clearer. Some trick of the construction turned the spiraling tunnel into a stone megaphone. With the knowledge that someone in the modern era had built at least the antechamber, Pat suspected the effect was intentional. At cardinal points around the central column of the spiral, more torches lit the way.

Throughout their descent, Pat kept his new spatial sense active, though well within the limits he'd painfully discovered. The staircase was really more of a ramp, as each stair wasn't more than a couple of inches high. Something else strange preyed on Pat's mind as they walked. The curves felt wrong. Off, as though they should have been steeper, but weren't. He shook it off and kept moving.

They passed through another arched doorway at the bottom of the spiraling staircase, this one blessedly free of mind-bending carvings, and entered a long room, oddly shaped room. Doorway opened up all along the wall, though upon investigation, they proved to be empty. Thankfully. Pat didn't want to face any more whacked out cultists than he absolutely had to.

Pat stopped in his tracks and cast about him. Something was off, wrong: he just couldn't quite tell what it was. Like an itch he almost felt. With a deep breath, and a quick prayer, he closed his eyes and pushed out with his new sense. The room *was* off. Lines curved when they should have run straight, and walls leaned in at angles that didn't make sense. When he pushed through the stone walls, his mind nearly cracked. On the other side stood dirt and rock and the remains of a civilization, and at the same time and occupying the same space, something both living and dead. And it knew he was there, as an elephant knew when a fly landed on it.

Pat's eyes sprang open, and he looked to Melody. Whatever she saw there lit a spark of fear in her azure eyes, a mirror of the sheer, atavistic terror that burrowed into Pat's bones.

"This whole place -" His voice cracked. Pat swallowed to ease his fear-parched throat and somehow forced words through his clenched jaws. "There's something - here. Something big. All around this place. Almost, like it's a part of it. We need to hurry."

Melody nodded, and Pat was impressed as she continued her soft singing. Together they turned toward the sound of the increasingly frenzied chanting coming out of one of the closer doorways.

As they approached, Pat saw the short passageway led into a cavernous room. Torches lit the sinister hallows with flickering flames that cast dancing shadows. The dimly lit space seemed filled with twisted pillars stone, all serpentine curves and sharp edges. Even as he moved, it seemed the pillars did, too. It quickly grew hard to gauge depth and distance.

They were lucky: they'd seen nobody in the disquieting temple. And a temple it was. Everything about it screamed place of worship. A twisted, evil sort of worship; worship of something horrific and unknowably cruel.

Pat slipped around a pillar and saw that getting noticed wasn't going to be a problem. just inside the pillars sat a crowd of people about Melody's age. Pat estimated no more than twenty, probably students by their dress, they sat in poses from rapt to bored. Pat marked that none of them bore the monstrous *Iaphneths*. Those were no doubt reserved for the chanters at the front of the sanctuary.

The half dozen celebrants in the room stood facing away from the entrance. Each one wore a deeply cowled garment covered in embroidered symbols that shrouded them from head to toe. They stood in a line at the front of the youths while a seventh figure stood in front of the black pool from Pat's nightmares. The leader of the unholy communion wore a robe like the others, but his head was bare, and Pat recognized Aram even though his back was turned.

Between them, on her back in the center of the ritual circle he remembered, struggled a young woman. Shackles held her arms over her head and her unclothed legs apart, and the monstrous eel-headed creature stood over her, vitriolic slime dripping from its open mouth. Pat remembered what Aram had said about Carla "being blessed for bearing the first of the New Ones."

The hooded figures twitched and writhed in their places. Pat's saw their robes squirming across the shoulders and his stomach turned again. Under each, he knew, lurked the clawed tentacular *Iaphneth.* Their hideous chanting rolled through the corrupt and darkened fane, and the crustaceous beast twitched in time to its rhythms.

An odd popping noise underlay the unholy scene. It wasn't until a chunk of the monster's chitinous plating fell off that Pat found its source. The thing was shedding its carapace, like some gargantuan insect. As he crept closer, Pat saw pale, pearlescent slime bubbling at the thing's serpentine neck.

In unison, the cowled celebrants lifted their arms, their chant rising to a fevered climax. With a roar, they wrenched their arms down to their sides. The figures slumped in fatigue, but Pat found his gaze locked on the creature. It's elongated head writhed on the column of its neck, fanged jaws snapping at the air. The popping noise increasing in volume and frequency, until it sounded like a machine gun. At last, the creature's armored hide disintegrated and sloughed off in a mass of purple shards.

As one, the young witnesses froze, and Melody gasped, shocked into silence. Pat couldn't fault them. The figure left behind only vaguely resembled the hulking arthropoid it had been a moment earlier.

Muscles writhed and bulged under the same blueish gray skin that covered its still-bestial head, the whole dripping with the slime of its horrific rebirth. It looked more manlike - though that wasn't hard - with its previously massive claws transformed into four long, opposable fingers. Its recurved legs now matched its arms in length, and as it rose to an alarming new height, a massive, barbed phallus depended from its groin.

Pat grimly raised his pistol, uncertain it would even help. At least the thing wasn't wearing an inch of armor anymore. Before he could squeeze the trigger, Aram turned around.

His robe was open to the waist, clearly displaying the horrific *Iaphneth* around his neck. He'd decayed from athletic-looking young student in the time since Pat had last seen him. He looked emaciated, his ribs standing out clearly under unhealthily gray skin.

The vile creature controlling the man, on the other hand, looked much like the one that had possessed Pat when it first cracked out of its egg. Fleshy tendrils the color of an ideal peaches-and-cream complexion wriggled on Aram's skeletal chest, interspersed with nightmarish, cherry-red claws halfway between fingers and a crab's legs.

The unholy combination of man and monster raised a bony finger to point right at Pat, and in a voice louder than he should have been able to manage, spoke.

"Apostate!"

Aram roared in his incomprehensible tongue, and froze Pat where he stood.

"You reject our fellowship, and then come to take what is ours by might? Our Mother will consume your soul for this affront!"

As a unit, the robed celebrants turned to face them, and Pat's mind nearly shut down. Mike had described what he'd looked like under the control of the *Iaphneth* Tourney killed, but Pat had pushed it away, suppressed it in the same way he'd tried to forget portions of that dark time.

Each of the robed figures bore an *Iaphneth*, and each had his or her head thrown back. Each horror thrust a muscular stalk out its host's mouth, grossly distending throats and jaws to the point of breaking, while tendrils and claws writhed around necks.

Pat wanted desperately to fall into a fetal curl, screaming at the horror facing him. A small, minuscule part of him, however, roared in the silence of his soul. All that he'd faced, all the Aram-*Iaphneth* and its pet monster had done to him, all that they still planned, and the weight of that horribly alien presence he'd felt. Everything that dreadful master of theirs wanted with its pawns and its tools and its victims.

All of it stopped now.

Pat raised his gun and centered the sights on Aram's furious face. The puppet shouted incomprehensible words that drove spike of pain through his head. His hands shook so much he couldn't aim properly, and Pat took his finger off the trigger for fear of shooting an innocent.

The hooded *Iaphneth* pawns spread out, moving through the small crowd of still-frozen witnesses. Pat took a momentary break in the agonizing incantations to duck behind a pillar, and saw Melody put her pipe to her mouth. Her song soothed the pain in his head and stilled his trembling hands. She looked at him and nodded. She'd been right, and Pat was going to apologize first thing, assuming they survived.

He spun around the other side of the pillar bare feet from one of the *Iaphneth*. The thing's horrible proboscis lunged toward him, fangs snapping. Pat whipped his gun up and squeezed the trigger, more by reflex than intention. The suppressor converted what should have been a deafening roar into a loud coughed, and the compact pistol sent a golden, glowing bullet through the thing's jagged-toothed maw.

The stricken monster flared its noisome appendages in its agony, before dissolving into a tarry goo that stained the robe of the man wearing it. The nameless man collapsed in a heap as the other *Iaphneth* howled in unholy chorus.

Pat's pulse pounded as he ducked behind another pillar. His bullet had *glowed*; he'd seen it appear to drift through the close air of the temple. And even though he'd been supremely lucky, he'd known the shot was good as soon as he felt the gun recoil.

On a hunch, Pat pushed out with his gifted spatial sense, nearly to his limits. He was rewarded with knowledge of just where everything in the room was. Aram still stood at the front of the room, and Carla was still chained to the ritual. Melody had moved away from him, still playing her blessed song. The abomination, on the other hand -

Pat's reflexes threw him into a diving roll as the monster's oversized hand smacked the pillar where his head had just been. Roll turned into scramble as the hissing creature followed him in bounding strides, doing its level best to crush him into red paste with its massive fists.

Aram screamed something that threatened to sink Pat's waking mind into the depths of insanity, but slid off the protective shield of Melody's music. Instead, the torches that lit the sanctum died, leaving Pat in an inky blackness, and giving him an uneasy revelation. The transformed horror glowed, a light blue like the skin of a corpse pulled from the water.

Pat gambled and closed his eyes, relying entirely on his gifted spatial sense to guide him. Adrenaline surged as he felt the thing just behind him and closing on its backward curved legs. Pat caught a pillar, and slung himself around it, throwing himself back in the other direction.

He kicked the thing in the leg as he went by. The thing's flesh gave more than he expected, and he almost tripped. He staggered, barely catching himself on another pillar. The monster roared, its hissing voice bell-like. He gained on it, leading him to believe he'd actually hurt the thing.

Aram shouted another command in his god's vile language, and Pat felt the remaining *Iaphneth* converge on Melody's location. As soon as they got to her, he knew they'd stop her song. Their rescue mission would be done for; the best outcome would be death. At worst, he'd be returned to that living death slavery, confined in the prison of his own mind. He didn't want to contemplate Melody's likely fate.

Pat screamed and sped up, weaving through the twisted columns. He drew deeply on his new senses, getting a feel for where his enemies were. He could almost see just where the monsters' grotesque limbs stretched out toward the spot where Melody hid.

Pat jinked to his left and ran toward the middle of the room. He slid to a halt and snapped his pistol up. At his shout, he sensed the *Iaphneth* puppets turn to face him. Pat trusted his newfound abilities and said a quick prayer.

His stubby pistol coughed once. Twice. Three time. Again and again once more. The slide locked back on an empty chamber. Five glowing rounds left brilliant tracks in the abyssal darkness, and he knew he'd shot well. He'd always been a good shot, but this verged on the ridiculous. Each shot took off a muscular, fanged pseudopod. Five bodies falling to the floor hit as one. Pat hoped they were still alive.

A hiss sounded in his ear, and the impact of a mighty arm lofted him into the still immobile students. Pat felt something crunch in his side, and waves of pain radiated out from his ribcage. He went down in a muddle of bodies, and lost his grip on his gun. Pat cast about him, but the shock of pain drove away his grasp of the surroundings.

Two softly glowing hands reaching into the mess and easily hefted Pat into the air. The jostling ground bits of broken rib together. Pat gasped, and immediately regretted it. Aram shouted a word and the torches flickered back into fitful life.

Pat's heart dropped. The kids he'd landed on hadn't moved. He had definitely broken at least one rib, and more importantly, lost his gun. And Melody was back there somewhere. In the relatively quiet moment, Pat heard Melody's song, still playing. The now-mournful notes comforted his fears, and actually seemed to sooth the shooting pain in his side.

The eel-headed monstrosity carried Pat over to the ritual circle, where he saw that Carla had passed out. Possibly from the pain of Aram's unspeakable commands, but likely from the sheer, sanity-shredding madness of the whole thing. He didn't blame her at all.

"Come out, girl," Aram sounded like a tired, old man. He'd aged even during the fight; his hair salt-and-pepper and his skin seamed with wrinkles. His thready voice sounded like he'd been gargling sandpaper, and he wheezed. "I have your ersatz hero, and if you do not show yourself, THIS INSTANT," he roared, and then fell into a coughing fit. "I will have my friend here pull him slowly limb from limb."

Melody stepped out from behind a pillar near the back of the sanctuary. Her azure eyes glowed in the torchlight, fairly spitting her hatred. Her fingers continued to weave magic from her penny-whistle.

"Your apostate," Aram spat, bloody saliva flying from his mouth in droplets, "will have to become my new host, I suppose." His mad, despairing eyes stared daggers at Pat and then shifted to Melody. "You will almost certainly qualify as a little mother, my dear."

The abomination holding Pat hissed.

Pat felt enough better from Melody's song that he tried his

senses. He pushed, just a bit, looking for his gun. He found it under the tangle of motionless students.

"Ahh, yes. My friend confirms that you're a virgin. He can taste such things in the air, you know. You'll have to wait a moon, but I'm sure we can fit you into our busy schedule. Our Mother will have a use for you." Aram leered at the young songstress. "Assuming of course, you survive the mating ritual."

Melody's face turned ugly, her skin flushing almost wine-red in the torchlight. Pat's still extended senses read the sudden surge of power in her, and his heartbeat sped up. She took her pipe from her mouth, her jaw dropped open, and then she screamed.

Her voice split, and split again, and then again. Pat could clearly hear each of the notes, combining in weird harmonies. His hair stood on end and his bowels shook. All the while his skull rattled with the force of her cry. By rights, the polytonal wave of sound should have shattered his eardrums. From the way Aram and his pet monster staggered, Pat guessed theirs had. The horror dropped Pat to the floor, then raised its head to the ceiling and shrieked.

Pat landed, fortunately on his good side, though it still hurt. As close to the stinking demon creature as he was, he swung a kick at its freakish member. Even without much force behind it, when Pat connected, it proved the thing was male, whatever it was. The beast's jaws snapped convulsively and it crashed to the ground. Its knees impacted the stone floor with an audible crack as Pat rolled out of its path.

Pat scrambled to get to his gun. Each shallow breath was an agony. Melody darted in and grabbed his arm, helping him to his feet. They staggered to the tangled knot of fallen students. Pat paused, sucking breaths just shallow enough to keep from sending jagged spikes into his side.

He'd just spotted his pistol when Aram started shrieking a chant in his unholy tongue. The room turned over, the pillars transforming into groping serpentine arms, reaching for them. This was on top of his sudden inability to form a coherent thought through the torment in his skull. He was distantly aware of Melody holding her head in her hands and screaming.

Suddenly, the torches burned a baleful blue, their flaring light leeching the color from the rest of the room. A pair of mottled black and green tentacles of terrifying proportion erupted out of the pool at the front of the sanctuary. One wrapped around the shrieking Aram-*Iaphneth,* while the other gripped the eel-headed creature in its powerful length. And then, they dragged their victims screaming into the water, which closed over them without a ripple. The torchlight faded back to normal.

Silence reigned, but for Pat and Melody's shuddering breaths. And then one of the students shifted. And then another. In moments, all of them moved about. Some sat with head in hands. Others stared at each other with wild eyes and vacant expressions.

Pat quickly ferreted his gun out of the mess. Despite the pain, he unscrewed the suppressor, swapped the empty magazine for a full one, and racked the slide. Carefully, he slid both the pistol and the suppressor into his shoulder rig.

His brain didn't seem to be working exactly. The whole experience was utter madness, of course. If it wasn't for the jagged pain in his side, Pat didn't think he'd have believe it actually happened.

One of the students came up to where Pat sat. He appeared to be in his early twenties, with light skin and curly reddish hair. He wore a polo shirt with an NYU symbol. He might well have been a friend of Aram's. Thoughts of the old-young man stabbed at Pat's chest with a very different kind pain than his broken ribs. He'd hoped he could save the kid.

"Uh, excuse me," the new kid said. He ran fingers through his hair. "Do, do you know where we are, Mister? Or how I got here?"

Pat blinked.

"Sure, man. We're under the Times Square subway station, but I have no idea how you got here." He looked for Melody, and snorted. He didn't need to look for her. He closed his eyes and felt for power. She was near the ritual circle, out of sight behind some of the milling kids. "Hey, could you grab a few of your buddies, and help that young lady over there?" Pat waved toward where he sense Melody crouching next to the still-unconscious Carla?

It didn't take much to get the students helping each other out of the temple. With Aram's rather sudden departure, and as Pat had already taken care of the other *Iaphneth,* nothing was there to stop them. Even the dreadful presence Pat had felt earlier seemed to have abated. Scared away, like as not.

Pat kept his breathing shallow. Without Melody's song, breathing hurt. Hell, sitting still hurt. While he kept his senses trained on the sanctuary room, Melody walked up and sat down near him.

"That is Carla," Melody confirmed. Her voice was nearly gone. Apparently, the super-scream of hers had a price. "She keeps asking where Aram is. Half the time, she's scared, and half the time furious. What should I tell her?"

"Tell her you don't know."

Melody looked at him.

"Do you?" she rasped.

He snorted and winced.

"One clue," he jerked his head in the direction of the dark pool, "but I'm not going in to find out."

Melody gave him a troubled look.

"Um, I looked at the pool. Unless there's a hidden door, it's only about six inches deep."

Pat turned to stare at her. A dozen half-thoughts ran through his head, but none of them came close to the surface.

"Well. That's a thing, isn't it?"

It took very little persuading to get the mess of students organized. Pat got them to carry the unconscious *Iaphneth* pawns up to the room in the abandoned subway station with the ladder up. A couple of women in the group helped Carla upstairs. Melody refused to go without him, which was a little weird.

Standing - hunched and in pain, but standing - near the ritual circle, Pat looked at the unpleasant fane. This was the same room he'd been held upon capture. The same room in which he'd been possessed by an evil alien intelligence. He was standing on the very spot, as a matter of fact. He saw no sign of the other *Iaphneth* eggs, though, and that bothered him. Six more of those things had hatched and taken hosts, but that was only six out of easily scores. Where had they gone?

"It's just us left, Patrick." Melody's roughened voice surprised him. She'd come up behind him without his noticing. He'd lost hold of his spatial sense from pain and exhaustion.

He looked around and saw she was right.

"We did good tonight, Melody," he said, and turned to hobble toward the way up. her expression dubious, she nevertheless nodded, then took his arm and drew it across her shoulders in tacit offering. Pat let her take some of his weight with gratitude.

Their walk up the spiral staircase and through the abandoned station was more of a shamble. They accomplished it in silence, each lost in private thoughts. At last, as they neared the ladder room, Melody looked up at Pat. Her drawn face had the same expression of long-held fear he'd seen in those who lived in gang-heavy neighborhoods.

"Patrick, what's really going on?"

He had no clue, but knew they needed to find out.

About the Author

David E. Pascoe is a ne'er-do-well of broad interests and little focus. He spent his childhood firmly ensconced in worlds of fantasy and science fiction with brief sorties into worlds of contemporary, horror and historical fiction of various stripes and inclinations. After rigorous intellectual training in theology and philosophy, he elected to enlist in the United States Navy, during which he used none of his skills to particularly good effect. Upon his separation from active duty, he dove back into science fiction, but this time as a writer. David spends his time in relative isolation somewhere on the East Part of the North American continent. His time is devoured by his son, a toddler, and his infant daughter, and caring for his wife. Writing has taken something of a back seat, a circumstance not to David's liking, nor to that of the characters occupying his head. They seem to be organizing a general strike...

www.ingramcontent.com/pod-product-compliance
Lightning Source LLC
Chambersburg PA
CBHW020411150626
46554CB00013B/686